Waiting for the Past

Middle East Literature in Translation
Michael Beard and Adnan Haydar, *Series Editors*

Select Titles in Middle East Literature and Translation

For a full list of titles in this series,
visit https://press.syr.edu/supressbook-series
/middle-east-literature-in-translation/.

Waiting for the Past

A Novel

Hadiya Hussein

Translated from the Arabic by
Barbara Romaine

Syracuse University Press

This book was originally published in Arabic as ما سيأتي (*Maa saya'ti*)
(Beirut, Lebanon: Al-mu'assasa al-Arabiya li-al-diraasa wa al-nashr
[Arab Institute for Research & Publishing], 2017).

First Edition 2022

22 23 24 25 26 27   6 5 4 3 2 1

∞ The paper used in this publication meets the minimum requirements
of the American National Standard for Information Sciences—Permanence
of Paper for Printed Library Materials, ANSI Z39.48-1992.

For a listing of books published and distributed by Syracuse University Press,
visit https://press.syr.edu.

ISBN: 978-0-8156-1151-6 (paperback)   978-0-8156-5574-9 (e-book)

Library of Congress Cataloging-in-Publication Data
Names: Ḥusayn, Hadīyah, author. | Romaine, Barbara, 1959– translator.
Title: Waiting for the past : a novel / Hadiya Hussein ;
translated from the Arabic by Barbara Romaine.
Other titles: Mā saya'tī. English
Description: First edition. | Syracuse, New York : Syracuse University Press,
2022. | Series: Middle east literature in translation
Identifiers: LCCN 2022023014 (print) | LCCN 2022023015 (ebook) |
ISBN 9780815611516 (paperback ; alk. paper) | ISBN 9780815655749 (epub)
Subjects: LCGFT: Novels.
Classification: LCC PJ7932.U77 M313 2022 (print) | LCC PJ7932.U77
(ebook) | DDC 892.7/37—dc23/eng/20220513
LC record available at https://lccn.loc.gov/2022023014
LC ebook record available at https://lccn.loc.gov/2022023015

Manufactured in the United States of America

*This translation is dedicated
to the memory of my father, William Romaine
(July 1, 1921–April 15, 2021).*

A wise man once said:
"In truth what hurts the tree is not the axe,
but that its handle is made of wood."

Contents

Acknowledgments

My thanks, first and foremost, to Hadiya Hussein, for the privilege of translating this novel. I express to Shakir Mustafa, friend and colleague, my heartfelt appreciation for endless patience and support through the process of bringing *Waiting for the Past* into its English rendition. Last but not least, profound gratitude to Maysaloun Faraj, who casts the light of her art upon a world in shadow, and has most generously given permission for the use of one of her extraordinary paintings to create the cover of this book.

Waiting for the Past

1

"To get there I'll open a thousand doors."

So Narjis said to herself, having sealed her lips, and from that time forward she began planning her escape, preparing for the long and exhausting journey: the journey that was to open for her other, unknown doors, confronting her with a life she had never yet known.

She was not entirely sure what would be the consequence of such an undertaking, nor could she have grasped it at the moment she decided to flee—it was all clouded. But she was driven by the forces of love and fear simultaneously, and she was determined to make the attempt, to try to achieve something better than just sitting and waiting for the final moment: death at the hands of forces outside one's own control.

When the time came, she packed a medium-sized suitcase, into which she put three shirts, a suit jacket, two skirts, two nightgowns, a towel, various toiletries including a toothbrush and toothpaste, and some underwear. She buttoned her blouse, then brushed her hair in front of the mirror and put it up in a ponytail, staring at her face, which was set with determination in those crucial moments, between one life on which she had closed the door and a different one she had not yet tasted. It might taste of honey or of bitter gourd, but she was prepared to swallow bitter gourd, or even poison, rather than stay as she was, prisoner of a barren life, stalked by fear from every direction.

She had already sold her mother's house—abandoned since she had inherited it—in order to finance her perilous journey. She had paid the sum upon which she and Mohsin al-Alwan had agreed, and would pay still more as circumstances required, in order that she might reach her destination. But why was Narjis fleeing, and where did she mean to end up? Where did she go, and what was it that she sought?

The first white ray of dawn crept gradually in to replace the black. The muezzin's voice, issuing from the mosque, summoned people to prayer, the words "Prayer is better than sleep" breaking like waves in his booming voice; she had not slept a wink. She felt no submissiveness as the imam, Nazih al-Amin, summoned the faithful: *Nazih al-Amin*, a name meaning "righteous and trustworthy," belonging to a man in whom Narjis discerned neither rectitude nor sincerity. She gazed from the upstairs window, which overlooked the street, until all the worshippers had made their way to the mosque and the street was empty of passersby. Her husband slept deeply in the other room, after his weekly night out, and as usual the rising sound of his snoring had found its way from one room to another. With the determination of a horse that will not be tethered to the earth, she slipped from the house, and inhaled the dirty air laden with the yellow dust of the khamsin.

On the previous day the temperamental desert, growing agitated, had blown about its densely particulate clouds, depositing their residue on all God's creation—humans, animals, and plants alike—invading the streets and houses and pounding them with waves of sand and dust, occluding the horizon and dimming the colors of the city. Then it subsided, leaving the atmosphere still enshrouded in dust.

There was a being, not human, its features indistinct, driving her powerfully in the borrowed voice of her mother. It came from somewhere beyond all that could be seen: "Where are you going, Narjis?" But she did not turn toward it—that voice could no longer stop her, and she felt no regret for what she had left behind. She knew that wagging tongues would stab her in the back, but this no longer concerned her. She had flung into the wastebasket everything that made up her past; now her time, her future, had commenced—still unclear, but with a bit of patience it would come clear enough. Something told her, "It's your turn now to seize the reins of your own destiny, to take matters in hand, and we'll be together all the way, for better or for worse."

She knew she would grow weary, and that the burden of her exhaustion would be hers alone to endure, on this journey that had cast her onto strange paths such as she had never trodden before, on which no one mattered to her but that man who still dwelt in her head and accompanied her steps, although she did not know whether he was alive or dead. All alone, unable to see clearly ahead of her, she faced the adventure or misadventure of a destiny spun from threads of fatigue and uncertainty: nothing ventured, nothing won, or what was the meaning of life? She would attain her object, armed with the proverb: "There is no destiny but that which we forge with our own hands."

The ends would justify the means—and yet, by what means was she to achieve her goal? Yes, from time to time she would complain, despair would pervade her soul and fear rend her heart, but in the end she would take courage, gird herself with patience, and be confident in the choice she had made. She would follow the stream whose springs had burst forth in her heart, to discover where it might lead.

What was Narjis seeking: for what purpose had she set out upon these rugged paths so fraught with peril?

2

Little by little the light advanced, dispelling what remained of the night's darkness before the sun overwhelmed it. It was dawn, the hour five-thirty, the air veiled in a layer of dust. Narjis was in a place called Nahdha Bus Terminal, her suitcase propped beside her. The white ribbon on its handle stood out conspicuously, a signal to the guide who would lead her on her journey of escape. She stared at the passing faces, and at those of the people positioning themselves for the start of a new day: women from the south, who sold clotted cream and honey, laying out their wares upon the floor. Small carts were set up, whose proprietors arranged goods for sale; beggars also took up their places to await the hands that might reach out to them. Many soldiers, too, were trying to get to their barracks, to resume those ceaseless wars, inevitably waged with these bodies snatched from the embrace of their mothers, their wives, their deferred aspirations. Their faces were etched with tribulation—they had had their fill, not of the world, but of sorrow; gunpowder clogged their noses as war effaced their dreams. They were, without doubt, expecting another war, from which how many of them would return? How many would lose a limb and be crippled for the rest of their lives? How many of their names would be erased from the annals? Oh, country, overflowing with oil, and yet hunger prevails: will your wars never end?

The time wore her down, dragging on for what seemed like ages—mocking her, lashing her with myriad fears and apprehensions. She was waiting for a certain person she had never laid eyes on, of whom she knew nothing except that he was a man, not very tall, wearing black trousers and a black-and-white striped shirt. His name was Abu Asim, and it was he who would take her to Khanaqin—so she had been told by Mohsin al-Alwan, who, well versed in smuggling operations, knew how to evade the hazards of the road. To his instructions he had added, "Don't initiate any conversation with him during the trip; wait until he speaks to you first."

She had not asked how the man would recognize her; before she could so much as open her mouth to inquire, he told her, as if he had read her mind, "He'll know how to find you. Bring a suitcase with a white ribbon tied to its handle, and put your hair in a pony-tail also tied with a white ribbon. Stand near the line of women selling tea and clotted cream. That's all you have to do, but—just to be sure—ask him his name before you go with him."

The hands of the clock seemed not to advance at all, but rather to retreat, so that she found herself squeezed by a monstrous pair of pliers—what if she should be caught? What reason could she adduce to justify her running away if they should arrest her and assail her with questions? Why, they would want to know, hadn't she notified the authorities of her departure from the city, since she had signed a pledge that bound her to stay? Who had instigated her escape? Where was she going, and what was she after? For whom was she working? Who was this Abu Asim, and what message was she carrying to deliver to the enemies of the state?

She felt as though her head would shatter with all these hypothetical questions, as still she stood there in Nahdha Bus Terminal, glancing occasionally at her watch and searching the faces around her. She realized that among the consequences of her running away was that it would create a resounding scandal in a closed society always eager for entertaining diversions: a protracted scandal, finding ready mouths to propagate it, to embellish the rumors, which repetition would convert to facts. But what else could she have done? Waste away and die a little more each day, simply to satisfy others? Or await her fate in the anteroom of one of the secret prisons?

Her situation would matter to no one but her husband, Mu'nis al-Shaa'ir,[1] and she was not afraid of him, dismissing as inconsequential his discovery

1. Shaa'ir, Mu'nis's surname, is also an Arabic lexical term meaning "poet."

of her running away—she did not even call it that; rather it was a search for a truth that was missing, and for a life of which she had dreamed but which she had never lived and must therefore seek elsewhere. Even once he found out what she had done, he would not be capable of quenching her rebellious spirit; all means of continuing under the same roof were closed to them now. During one of their many quarrels, she had driven him to make a verbal declaration of divorce, for she knew that the way through the courts was long and exhausting. The decision to leave had come over her as soon as she discerned the merest ray of light to guide her: a faint beam, spun from a fragile hope that left her no alternative.

No, with regard to her husband her conscience would not trouble her. He had within minutes retreated from his decision to take the oath of divorce, and tried in various ways to make amends, but she would not accept his retraction. Although her husband had come to his decision in the heat of the moment, it was she who had devised it; she had seen her opportunity and goaded him into a hasty declaration, as if she had been awaiting her chance since the day she married him. What mattered to her now was that, before God, she was free of this man, a stranger to her body, husband to her only in the eyes of others. Her mother, who had ensnared her in this marriage, no longer had any authority over her, for she had succumbed to death several months earlier. Nor did her relatives have any influence, for all contact with them had been severed when her father was killed in the war.

Her real fear, the dread that taxed her endurance of the passing time as she stood there in Nahdha Bus Terminal, was something else, subject to the law of the land: the law that, closing its myriad talons on the populace, controlled people's lives to the point where no one dared speak openly of politics, for fear of an eavesdropping neighbor, or even a family member secretly in the service of the government agents, who might report to them something overheard. Should they discover the intention behind her flight, she would be at the mercy of the four winds. She could not tell what might become of her or what torture she might have to withstand so as not to confess—this for the sake of those who had paved the way for her escape, after a security officer had forced her to sign a paper that bound her to give information if anything new came to light in connection with Yusef Hassan Omran; the document bound her also to stay where she was or, should she decide to travel to another city, to inform the authorities and declare the purpose of her journey.

After a period of time that seemed endless, she was roused from her reverie by the short man's voice: a voice high as a note played by the wind in the reeds. Standing beside her, not looking in her direction, he said, "Madame Narjis?" Her breath seemed to stop when she heard her name, and her pulse raced. She glanced briefly at him—he looked more dwarf-like than merely short-statured, lost in his voluminous striped shirt, his head set between sloping shoulders, his hair thick and black as a toupee.

"What is your name?" she asked him.

"Abu Asim," he replied.

How, she wondered privately, is this diminutive fellow going to protect me from the dangers all around me? Before making any move, he said to her, "Follow me."

Putting some distance between herself and him, she followed him to a taxi parked a few meters away. Its driver was standing beside the hood, a light-complexioned man with a thin gray moustache, wearing a faded blue dishdasha and a red-and-white checked kaffiyeh.

Next to a window in the back, behind the driver's seat, sat a woman who appeared to be in her sixties, of dignified mien but with an expression of deep misgiving. She was slight, of light-brown complexion with a scattering of freckles. She wore a long dress, black with white dots, over which was a black abaya, and her hair was covered by a black shawl. In her hand was a string of brown prayer beads. Narjis seated herself by the window on the other side, behind her guide, the short man. Tugging at the white ribbon in her hair, to release the ponytail and let her coal-black hair flow over her shoulders, she leaned back to rest against the seat.

The car set out, the driver's hoarse voice invoking God's protection, "In the name of the one, the only, and with his blessing," words that brought calm to Narjis's spirit—albeit a calm pierced from time to time by her doubts about what she was facing. She did not relax entirely until the car had passed through one of the gates of Baghdad beneath a tent-like vault of dust—leaving behind dozens of murals depicting the man who held everything in his grasp, including the souls of his people—and merged onto the highway, which had murals likewise on display for many miles.

Lost in thought, Narjis wondered, "Shouldn't the millions expended on erecting these murals all over the country, north to south and east to west, have been spent on providing for all the poor people living in squalor?" Then she was assailed by a sense that the man pictured on the murals was pursuing her and might pelt her with stones no matter which way she turned, in order to send her back to where she'd started.

Hastily she drove this thought from her mind, lest it possess her, and turned her attention to the section of the back seat that held no third passenger. How could a driver go anywhere without his full complement of fares? Perhaps the older woman was thinking the same thing. Uneasy, Narjis turned to the other passenger, but found her just then directing her gaze toward the road on the other side.

Whenever the car traversed a long stretch of empty road, the sense of calm receded from Narjis's heart, making way for her apprehensions as to what might happen before they reached Khanaqin. She tried to dismiss from her imagination visions of the police car that would bring her back, not to her home, but to one of the innumerable dimly lit rooms at police headquarters. There would be a gleam in the eyes fixed on her by the interrogating officer, the same leer that had shamed her when she was interrogated after Yusef disappeared. Now she pushed that face away and turned to the woman sitting next to her—perhaps a conversation between the two of them would give her some peace of mind. But the woman did not turn her head, nor did so much as a word or a murmur escape her lips—there was only the movement of her fingers on the string of brown prayer beads as, perhaps, she recited her prayers in silence.

The sun flooded the earth and its denizens with blinding light—in a matter of hours the radiant ball would intensify its heat, scourging all creatures, for it was the middle of June. The diaphanous layer of dust dwindled gradually away, and an hour later Narjis was overcome by nagging anxieties of another sort, for the two men had started conversing in Kurdish, or possibly Turkmen—she knew neither language, but she knew both were used in the north. What was going on? Why were they talking in a different language when both of them could speak Arabic? Moreover, the short man, her guide, did not look like a Kurd—his features gave him away, announcing his rustic southern origins, notwithstanding his city attire. All sense of reassurance fled, as alarm closed in on her. From time to time she turned to the passenger beside her, but the woman seemed to be in another world, seated rigidly in her place, wrapped up in some concern of her own. She had stopped fingering her prayer beads. Each time Narjis looked at her, her face presented an enigma, revealing nothing. Perhaps she, too, was running away from something, and was sufficiently preoccupied to be oblivious to the men. Her only gesture was to wipe the sweat from her face with the edge of her black shawl.

The terrain was no longer flat, but undulating, the horizon opening onto a void, the land stretching out in both directions empty of houses, farms, and humans: a wasteland but for thorn bushes, the husks of burned-out vehicles, and desiccated trees still in their places, dead perhaps from thirst in the merciless heat of summer. From time to time Bedouin hair-tents would appear in the distance, or mud-brick houses, the car passing once more into a desolate landscape as soon as it left these behind. All the while the men carried on their conversation, uninterrupted, in some other language, and fear enveloped Narjis once more, but whether all this made any impression on the silent woman beside her she had no way of knowing.

Narjis felt the trickle of sweat from her armpits and beneath her ears. Then at last the other woman, who had not uttered a word this whole time, opened her mouth. Addressing the driver as she mopped the sweat from her brow, she said, "Doesn't this car have air-conditioning?"

"It's broken," came the reply, as sharp and dry as the summer climate of this country. He said nothing more, and the woman made no comment, except to grumble and lapse once more into silence. Narjis, meanwhile, was beset by memories of people's faces: the face of her mother when she upbraided Narjis; Yusef, who had vanished without a trace; her husband, who at this moment appeared balloon-like, flushed and bloated with fury; and finally, persistently, the face of the interrogating officer, who had practically undressed her with his leering glances.

"A woman like you—beautiful, desirable . . . why would you associate with a traitor?"

She made no reply.

"Was there no one else you found attractive, no one else who could satisfy your desires?"

She held her tongue.

"The love story's over—forget about it. Look for an honorable man."

Her lips trembling, she spoke. "What did Yusef do that made him a traitor? He doesn't even own any weapons."

"Haven't you heard the old saying? 'Your tongue is your horse; gives good service if you're nice, but repays abuse with abuse.' The tongue is more dangerous than a gun. If you weren't the daughter of a martyr, and if your mother weren't ill, I would deal differently with you. As it is, I'll let it go with a warning—this time. Next time you'll pay dearly for it if you don't cooperate. Read this and sign it."

She did as she was told, thinking he'd be satisfied with that, and waiting for him to dismiss her. Instead he stared at her chest, where her cleavage would be, deliberately, so as to mortify her; she reached for the buttons on her blouse, thinking one of them must have come undone. He laughed at her.

"You have a direct and binding agreement with me," he said, "not to hide any information about Yusef that you may receive. It is imperative you understand that your movements will be watched, and that there are no secrets we have ever failed to expose." He dismissed her with a wave, but then he added, "You are forbidden to leave Baghdad except at my command—understood?"

His telephone rang, and no sooner had he picked it up than he raised his voice . . . but the memory of his shouting dissolved as the car began to shudder.

The driver stopped the car and got out. "What's going on?" Narjis's question slipped out, addressed to no one in particular. She looked at her diminutive guide—perhaps he would turn and reassure her. She saw his head, sunk between his shoulders, with no discernible neck, turn only to the right as he opened the door and got out, without facing the two women or even casting so much as a glance at Narjis. She turned to the other woman, and saw alarm in her eyes, but the woman uttered not a word. Instead, she started looking from one side of the road to the other, where no one was to be seen. Then she turned to Nar-jis, just as they heard the voice of the driver, who had stuck his head in the driver's side window.

"Get out of the car," he said.

His voice was jarring—hoarse, like a sound produced by a predatory beast—and Narjis felt the blood drain from her face, as must no doubt have happened as well to the woman beside her. They did not move until the driver summoned them a second time: "Get out of the car—we've had a breakdown."

They got out and stood side by side, some distance from the men, and then Narjis heard the words, "God help us." She didn't know whether it was she or the older woman who had spoken, she was so frightened. Fear had got the better of her, paralyzed her. The place was empty and bleak, the terrified eyes of the women fixed on the men lest they should make any move that might alter the course of this journey and their own fate. What had the driver intended by ordering them to get out of the car, claiming it had broken down?

No cars passed by, and no buildings could be seen. The parched land looked flat, an extension of the sky, but without a smidgen of blue: a trackless waste in which the only refuge was oblivion. Here and there it appeared cracked with thirst; elsewhere it was sandy and punctuated by rocks. The hot wind flung indistinct echoes at the menacing void: the voices of wandering ghosts, perhaps, come to see what would happen—for there was no one around but the four of them. Narjis noticed that the other woman was once more fingering her prayer beads, and that she was chanting the Qur'anic verse, "The Throne," never taking her eyes off the two men. Narjis clutched the woman, who turned to her, her face full of an apprehension she could not conceal.

"Don't be afraid," the woman said. "If the Devil tempts them, do as I tell you."

Narjis grew paler still, her eyelids twitching and chest heaving with anxiety. Where was the courage that had washed over her when she resolved to flee? Where was the cavalier defiance that had inspirited her? She was being tested for the first time, and looking weak in the face of challenge. How would she ever be able to open the thousand doors in such a state of fear, terror showing in her eyes?

The other woman spoke again uneasily, after glancing at the two men, who were taking turns addressing themselves to the problem with the car.

"While I live," she said, "they won't take advantage of you. I'll defend you to the death."

With that she once again took up reciting "The Throne" in a low voice.

Narjis could not settle her mind; as her anxieties mounted, the color of her face reflected the various forces that agitated her. What if the other woman should die at the hands of these unknown men— would her turn be next? Would they rape her, then kill her, and bury the two bodies here beneath the vault of the sky, in the blazing sun? Had she come here to die on this godforsaken ground, having scarcely begun her journey, much less attained the goal that was its object? Was it possible that Mohsin al-Alwan had colluded with the government agents, and, in sending this dwarf-like man to her, ensnared her in a trap of which Mukhlis Farouq knew nothing? Or had Mukhlis Farouq misjudged her and failed to understand Mohsin al-Alwan's intentions as well? In such a time as this, anything was possible when nothing was reliable.

And why, in this annihilating heat, were her teeth chattering?

During this interval the short man had gone off some distance to a spot that was lower than the surface of the road. Stepping behind a camel's-thorn bush, he ducked his head, his hands evidently busy unbuttoning his trousers so that he could urinate. Only the upper half of his body could be seen—his black-and-white-striped shirt and his hair, thick and black like a wild donkey's. Like someone seeking greater protection, Narjis clutched the older woman more and more tightly, warily observing the men, as if danger from all sides was now imminently upon them. The short man emerged once more from behind the camel's-thorn bush and spat twice on the ground. He walked back toward the vehicle to give a hand to the driver, who stood at the hood of the car, examining its innards.

After about ten minutes, the driver lifted his head and gestured toward the two women to come and help push the car. Cautiously they approached, while the short man took hold of the passenger's side front door and the driver sat at the wheel to operate the engine. Hot winds animated the dry air, spinning here and there in little funnels that stirred up the dust and dropped it on their faces. From time to time Narjis cast a glance at the short man, in the hope that he might convey some reassurance or, on the other hand, she might discern from his expression any dirty trick at which he could have connived with Mohsin al-Alwan, who had thrown her to an evil fate directed by a man who, by God's will, was a dwarf.

Although the men had made no alarming moves, the women were still far from reassured. Each of them thought that the breakdown of the car, and hence the necessity to push it, could be a ruse on the part of the men, to establish false trust; nevertheless, they pushed, without relaxing their wary vigilance. The car moved very slowly and then, little by little, speeded up. They all resumed their seats to continue the journey.

The driver spoke, addressing his diminutive passenger this time in Arabic. "Along this route there's a mechanic," he said. "Let's hope the engine won't fail again before we get there."

The women's fear had not yet dissipated, for it might be that the men had talked matters over between them, arranging to carry out their plan for the women in some other place. The car progressed in fits and starts, until, in the distance, a dilapidated building appeared, perched all alone beneath the infinite sky. It was the mechanic's workshop, and there the car came to a stop. It was an elongated building of dark gray cinder block, with a corrugated roof. A boy stood in the doorway, and inside sat a man of about forty, smoking and drinking tea. Once more everyone got out of the car.

The older woman looked around for a lavatory. Failing to see any sign of one, she approached the boy, who was near the car, to ask him where she might attend to her need. He pointed toward the back of the building, and she, by now clutching her stomach, hurried in the direction he had indicated. Narjis followed her.

There was a pit in the ground, walled off with cinder block, but unroofed. In a corner of the enclosure sat a bucket, which held water; there was also an upside-down metal pot, and a green plastic pitcher that was turning black from accumulated filth. This was what passed for a latrine. But there was nothing for it except to make do, so the older woman went first, while Narjis waited her turn. The earth was enveloped by silence and flooded with blazing sunshine. There were crows, some in flight, some alighting on the rocks, and still others digging in the ground. The silence engulfing Narjis resounded in her chest.

The woman came out of the latrine, so that Narjis could quickly take her turn. Repelled by the squalor of the place, she wasted no time there.

The older woman was still an unknown quantity, a box with its secrets sealed inside. Perhaps she thought of Narjis the same way, but the two of them exchanged a few words, talking about the problem with the car, and how far they still had to go before reaching Khanaqin. When Narjis asked about this, the woman replied, "We're two-thirds of the way there."

Understanding from these words that the woman knew the way well, Narjis added, "Are you from Khanaqin?"

The woman shook her head. "No," she said, "I'm from Baghdad. I'm going to my sister's house in Khanaqin. And you?"

The question threw Narjis into confusion. What had she meant to say to her as she opened her mouth? The voice of the driver cut in at the same moment. "It's time," he said. "We'll be on our way soon." Her lips had moved, in search of something—anything, perhaps—that she might say.

Now the other woman moved forward; Narjis followed her, and they waited a little way from the door to the workshop. The woman sat cross-legged on the ground, despite the heat it gave off, reciting prayers for safety. She did not repeat her question to Narjis—it was as if she had forgotten it entirely or had never asked it in the first place. Narjis, for her part, remained standing. They exchanged only a few words about the situation with the car, the woman calling upon God to take pity on them and resolve the problem before it got dark. At the word "darkness," Narjis was seized by fear.

"How would we get through this," she asked, "if darkness fell?"

The woman grimaced. "We would leave matters in God's hands," she said, "for he is the one who knows our predicament."

Narjis felt her heart contract. How she wished that, on this fearful journey, she might tell her cares to this woman, finding in her a sympathetic listener and lightening her burden. But on hearing these words spoken by the woman, she was seized with despair—seized and struck mute.

Time passed in a silence that grew and stretched until it was broken by the short man, who spoke to them with a rasping in his throat. "The problem is solved—you can get in the car." He gestured to them to take their places in the vehicle. In a voice broken by sadness the older woman said, as she steadied herself with her right hand on the ground and got to her feet, "Lord, our fate is in your hands."

The terrain began again to undulate, and to rise. Hills, creased and furrowed, could be seen, as well as bushes and houses, widely spaced—and still they had a long way to go.

How could you have entrusted yourself, Narjis, to a man you didn't know, merely on the strength of a promise with nothing behind it, apart from a scrap of paper originating who knows where?

3

I am Narjis, my mother's only child; I am a woman of fear kept hidden for thousands of years, distilled by women who left this life before they could realize their dreams. From childhood the seed of fear was implanted deep within me, growing and flourishing on I know not what. Dark and closed off places terrified me; I often cried and clung to my parents if I found myself in a dimly lit corner; the light in my room was left on all night, to ward off the ghosts that would otherwise attack me, emerging from behind the curtains and doors, or from the branches of trees in the garden by the house: enormous phantoms with glowing eyes, long noses, and tails of fire. I would cry out in agony, as if bitten by a viper, if the light went out. My mother tried to rid me of my phobia of dark places, making me confront the terror that possessed me so that I could see for myself that there was no such thing as ghosts— she would seize hold of me forcefully, attempting to run with me toward the dark corridor at one end of the house. "Stop screaming," she would say to me, agitated, "there aren't any ghosts in the shadows."

Weeping, I would reply, "I saw the ghosts coming from the garden!" And when I kept on screaming, my father would come, gather me in his arms, and take me to the garden, where he would approach the trees, telling me of the gentle birds that were asleep in the branches, that there were no ghosts except the ones in my young mind. Then my mother would come outside as well and take me, kindly this time, caressing my trembling body and dabbing at my tears. I would sob against her chest until I fell asleep, and then she would put me to bed, leaving the door open as she went out of the room.

When my life hung upon the boughs of early adulthood, the age of a woman in the bloom of youth, my face was round and rosy-cheeked, eyes deep brown, body well-proportioned, mind infused with an obstinacy deriving from my mother's genes, although my willfulness always yielded to the rock of her own obduracy—not from fear of her, but as a matter of love and respect for her.

Now that youthful charm no longer matters to me. The well of my emotions has run dry at an early age, with my loved ones all gone, and myself still wrapped in a cloak of fear that will pursue me with every step I take, although it won't break my determination to persist until I arrive at my goal, no matter how much the endeavor costs me. How can fear and stubbornness coexist? Isn't this contradictory? So it seems to me—sometimes I feel that I am a woman of contradictions, but this is difficult for me to interpret.

Perhaps when my mind is put at ease and can settle, I will know this woman who has taken possession of me; or perhaps not. That is not the important thing, as long as she is, now, on the point of this journey whose end cannot be known. I will be sustained by the memories I carry in my head, and perhaps they will help shorten the distance and mitigate, if only a little, the fear that has rooted itself in my viscera.

Who was it, Narjis, who called you "Narjis"? How frequently I was asked this question! I answered as one who took pride in a precious thing: "My father chose my name, and in his fondest moments he says to me, 'My little narcissus!'" My father left this world with the first round of conscriptions for the war, leaving his little narcissus to a mother who feared for her daughter at the slightest breath of wind, and grew harsher toward her with every inch she grew. Her severity was born of her own bereavement just when she was in her prime; her being robbed of the body of the man she loved, my father, whom the war had shattered, and there was no way for her to know whether the body that came back was entirely his, or whether it was an assemblage of parts cobbled together from the collective dead, for she was not permitted to open the sealed coffin.

I was twelve years old at the time. My mother visited my father's grave regularly, until there came a day when she stopped going to the cemetery, the day she returned trembling, all color drained from her face, and told her friend Rabab that she had been confounded at hearing a wordless clamor issuing from the grave, causing her to turn around in case her ears had deceived her, picking up the voices of people in a corner of the graveyard. But the place was empty of any living souls that day, and when the noises began to grow louder the shock sent her fleeing headlong, stumbling among the graves, hearing footsteps in pursuit of her—it sounded like many feet following her.

Could it be that those voices belonged to the body parts that had been jumbled together from multiple bodies and interred along with those of my father? My mother thought so, too. She stopped visiting the grave, not only because she was terror-stricken, but because now she had confirmation of her conjecture, that this grave was not my father's alone, but was shared by other men, and she could spare enough sorrow only for one.

My mother was an attractive woman, her beauty manifest in the proportions of her body, the shine in her lovely eyes, her tanned complexion; she exuded the most alluring charms. She suffered the louche attention of men—the imam of the mosque, no less, Nazih al-Amin—whose stares penetrated her clothing. There were those who whispered unceasingly when the imam approached her, the smell of his maleness emanating from him. It only got worse after my father was killed, for here was this enchanting woman, now deprived of a man's warmth. This was before her condition was altered in an instant by the violent fate that robbed her of one of her beautiful eyes, taken by shrapnel from an explosion, which left a scar on her left cheek and, at the corner of her lips on the same side, a spherical swelling that, when she spoke, moved in such a way as to resemble a morsel of food being chewed.

What a reversal for my mother—that day, on which her life was so changed. Even the death of my father didn't affect her as that day did. I was coming home from school, and caught up in exultant fancies, for I carried with me an award, a certificate of outstanding performance. I got off the bus and crossed the main road; I had a ten-minute walk before the turnoff onto our street, but no sooner had I crossed the main road and gone a few steps than there was a terrifying explosion close to the police station. It was my mother's ill fortune to be nearby at the moment of the blast. I ran toward the house, but I couldn't get to it. Amid the screaming and the wailing and the blood was the shriek of sirens—fire and ambulance, a deafening uproar. Security forces set up a barrier, prohibiting anyone from approaching the spot. I heard a voice I couldn't recognize: "Narjis, go to your mother in the ambulance." I screamed and pushed my way forward, pleading with the police officers and firemen; I found myself jammed against bloodied victims, amidst their weeping and moaning, the cries and the blood, and I scarcely recognized my mother, severed that day from a woman's dreams, from that fascinating self whose allure seemed to emerge from the pages of a picture album.

Once her face was disfigured, she no longer opened the album, nor did she ever look in mirrors. Adding to her torment, there were people who would avoid crossing her path when they saw her, who would murmur and mutter, superstitious about the evil eye with which they believed such a defect was associated. Even Nazih al-Amin, the imam, who held forth at the Friday prayer, exhorting the people to conduct themselves righteously, would move away when he caught sight of her, although previously he had lusted after her. If he was caught off guard at finding her near him, he would turn his face away and recite, as if he had seen the Devil, "Say: I seek refuge in the lord of Paradise from the evil he created"—never mind that what God had created in her had been most beautifully formed, and that what happened to her was the work of no creator, but of human devils.

The exception was her friend Rabab, who was steadfast in her attendance on my mother throughout the days she spent in the hospital, and remained loyal to her. She did not change just because my mother's appearance had, but behaved as if my mother had undergone no disfigurement. When they spoke together, Rabab did not focus on her facial features or fixate upon the movement of the little round protuberance that moved just behind the left side of her mouth, or upon the left eye, extinguished, no longer able to see the light.

That accident destroyed her life. The only compensation she could find for her sufferings was to meddle in my life . . ."Where are you going, Narjis? Don't be late. You don't know the power of your looks—some charmer will seduce you. Be careful, Narjis, your dress is too short. And what is this lipstick, and this rouge on your cheeks? God didn't stint you for beauty, did he, with those cheeks like ripe fruit, those lips like cherries? Don't wear your hair loose like a gypsy, restrain it and put it in a braid—people will respect you more."

Whenever my mother looked at me, I knew before she opened her mouth what she wanted to say to me—I had memorized her speeches, which remained with me like a ringing that penetrated my head and splintered my ears. Sometimes I spoke first, repeating her phrases back to her, laughing, and then she would add even more, all manner of advice: "I'm afraid for you, my girl—and what will people say about me? 'She doesn't know how to raise her daughter'? It's exhausting, bringing up girls with no man around. Your father was decent and honorable—there's no one to rival him in that except my brother, your Uncle Bandar, who's taken himself off and I don't know where in the world he's gone."

I couldn't accept this comparison between my father and my uncle, whose features faded from my mind long before my mother quit comparing them, when my uncle returned so changed in his appearance. My father had been elegant and fastidious, a man of good taste and calm demeanor. All I can recall of my uncle, on the other hand, is that he was a troublemaker, garrulous and excitable, with no sense of refinement. He had emigrated years before to America, declaring, like a slogan, "My freedom first and foremost," although he wasn't being persecuted by the authorities. His ideas were vague, nonspecific. News of him stopped coming, and his image grew in my mother's mind, overflowing more day by day with a sanctity he had not earned—until one day when there came a knock on the door, and we opened it to find a bearded man wearing a jubbah and a turban.

We thought he was a beggar or a person soliciting donations for the mosques or someone who had, perhaps, got the wrong address. Then he cried out joyfully to my mother, "Salma, my sister! It's Bandar!" He had recognized my mother despite her distorted features. Her jaw dropped, and she stared at him in disbelief. Once she was sure he really was her brother, she put her arms around him.

He stayed in our house for about an hour, was served tea twice, and talked about the light that had burst forth from within him, guiding him on his path to God in a different part of the world. He didn't offer any details about this light. Then he went away, saying he wanted to visit a friend of his in Babel and, if he had time, he would come back again to see us. Before he got as far as the door, he turned to me and said, "Daughter of my sister, don't bar your own way to God's paradise—cover your head to gain entrance there." I had nothing to say to this.

It seemed his schedule didn't permit him to visit us again, for we didn't see him thereafter. He spoke to my mother by telephone, saying his time had run short, and he must return to America. Meanwhile, the question hung on my lips: How was it that he had come back from the land of "freedom" bearded, wearing a jubbah and a turban?

My mother was wasting away, day by day, as illness ravaged her. Her condition had been diagnosed as stomach cancer, which ate away at her even though she adhered conscientiously to her regimen of chemotherapy drugs. Her condition worsened, and when there was a shortage of drugs available at the hospitals, she felt sure her fate was sealed. Nothing mattered to her anymore, other than what would become of me. Once again she was like a broken record on the subject of getting me married off. She nagged and wept, and in the midst of her agonies she reminded me of her imminent end: "I'm afraid I'll die before you get married—why don't you marry, Narjis, and set my mind to rest?"

"Mama, I'm engaged to the man I love, who's disappeared. You know this."

I said these words to myself—I didn't dare say them out loud to her, for had I done so she would have gasped in alarm. She might have screamed, and beaten her head against the wall, the knot under the flesh of her jaw on the left side rotating more than ever as she pushed her words out, scattering them, then gathering them together in one cry:

"How can you still be in love with a fugitive, a wanted man? Isn't it enough, what you went through at the police department?"

And maybe I would tell her that they had disappeared him, that he was not a fugitive, for what had he done that he should have to run away?

She would reply, "Then he's been done away with, and in that case you need to get on with your life. Have you ever seen anyone come back from the dead? Or do you want to let one of the authorities make an easy meal of you? I won't rest in my grave, daughter. I'll be tormented—will it make you happy, knowing that I'm in torment? Isn't the anguish I've suffered in life enough?"

She'd say more than this, too. She'd weep buckets and rake her face with her nails—her face, already ruined by shrapnel. So I'd hold my tongue, think twice about my words before my tongue got loose and confided the designs of my heart. I offered a reply meant to reassure her.

"When destiny comes calling, Mama, there is no evading it."

The lines in her face smoothed out, as she grew calmer, saying, "I keep telling you, Narjis—your destiny is right before your eyes. Don't waste your chance."

It was Mu'nis al-Shaa'ir she meant, the son of her friend Rabab. She wanted to repay the care Rabab had extended to her through her afflictions, and marry me to Mu'nis, a man bloated with his own self-regard.

We both fell quiet, she awaiting my answer, and I lamenting my predicament. When the silence between us lengthened, she said, her eyes full of entreaty, "What will your life be like after I'm gone, daughter? I don't believe I will ever rest in my grave if I leave you on your own."

I married Mu'nis al-Shaa'ir, who afterward made use of my body, but remained ignorant of my mind and my feelings. I set the condition that I should not have to live in a lofty apartment such as the one his mother lived in on the ninth floor of the Salhia Complex, so he rented for me a ground-floor apartment in a nearby building, in order to stay close to his mother. I married him to fulfill the wishes of my mother, whose death I was expecting, envisioning my crushing loneliness in her absence. I accepted him as my husband to satisfy her, to grant the final wish of her life. Then I divided my time between her and my husband, not finding in him a man who could please me or possess me. I felt no warmth from his hands, no frisson from his touch; I didn't feel the electricity of love surge through my body the way it had with Yusef at the merest touch of his fingers. In an attempt to rouse my senses, Mu'nis undertook the impossible; they did not stir, and I achieved no harmony with him. Our bodies repulsed each other, and in bed with him I found that I was nothing but a corpse awaiting its interment in the ground. Each time he touched me, I was overwhelmed with a sense of being contaminated, always feeling that I was pledged to another man, for whom I would wait my whole life. Sometimes I would be startled, when I woke up late at night and found a man sharing my bed, but in the next moment I would remember that I was married. It was bizarre that Mu'nis would demand that I love him as he loved me, as if love were a commodity to be purchased from the perfumeries, or as if it were some sort of substance stocked with the pharmaceutical supplies, with which he had only to anoint my body and it would blaze with love, aflame with desire. With him I was always colder than February's chill. Only with someone we love can that flame be lit.

What was I to do, not seeing in him a man equal to my dreams as Yusef was? Finding in him only a man to whom life had not granted the chance to live up to his name, a man who fancied himself a figure of importance each time he wrote a poem, who dreamed of appearing one day on the television screen, who forced his way into every social occasion so that he could recite his silly poetry, who felt elated by the laughter of the audience? I smiled bitterly whenever they would laugh, charmed by his poems—foolishness rendered up by a fool. "What nonsense is this that he's spouting?" I would say to myself. I pitied him and myself. Too often he would press me for my opinion after reciting some of his poems to me when we were alone, and I would suppress the smile hovering on my lips and tell him, "It's you who's the versifier—*I* don't understand poetry." Then he would get angry and tell me I was ignorant.

And so, day by day, the chasm between us grew wider and deeper, until I could no longer abide his breathing next to me in bed, his offensive exhalations of garlic and strong spirits. Everything in me had died, and his efforts to charm me could not stir that still pond within me. Why had my mother died a mere handful of weeks after my marriage? Had she held off her death in order to make certain I first passed into the custody of a man, so that her soul would be at peace? My mother passed away satisfied with me, leaving me bereft of satisfaction with myself. She died, with her mutilated face; afterward it was my life that was mutilated.

One night, when he came home drunk from a night out with his friends—and I knew there was no end to his self-indulgence—I had slept fitfully, as I often did. Sometimes he would creep into bed, trying not to wake me, and I would know from the odor of his body, like the smell of a smashed watermelon, that he had exhausted his energy while he was out. On this particular night, however, he tried deliberately to wake me. He was riled up like a bull, his breath coming fast and hard, his fingers probing my body, seeking out particular spots. There was nothing I could do but push his hands off and edge away from him in the bed. "Stop it!" I shouted at him, as if I'd been stung by a scorpion. The veins stood out in his forehead and he went red in the face, still trying to get at me, with no regard for the anger in my voice, hoping to elicit the breath of life in the corpse that shared his bed. Failing to get what he wanted, he began to beg me, his breath smelling of *araq*. It was the first time I had seen him this way, so weak and so abject, but all the same I felt no pity for his helplessness—I felt contempt, rather, for his self-abasement. Once more I shouted at him, "Don't touch me!" I gathered my nightshirt around my body and prepared to get out of bed. In a pleading tone, spraying my face with droplets as he spoke, he said, "What's going on with you? Have you become so completely unfeeling?"

I nearly laughed out loud at the irony, and said "What would you know about 'feelings'? You with the sensibilities of a 'poet'? Are your feelings all about what's between your legs?" But I didn't say this. I got out of bed, holding back a cri de coeur. When I left him he didn't try to follow me, but I heard his abuse, obscenities falling from his flaccid, drunken mouth. I said no more than, "Sorry—there's nothing I can do for you," and I went to the room where I would take refuge whenever I grew sick and tired of him.

It was true: there was nothing more I could do. I couldn't manufacture love to fit the measurements of my husband, whom I did not love—the volcano that was my body rose up in rebellion. Beginning that night, an actual rupture began to form. Supposing that this was the definitive moment, there was then a period during which each of us did everything possible to achieve our opposing goals. His was to please me, as he still thought that the reason I was so distant and so cold toward him was grief for my mother's death; thus he persisted in his belief that in time this would run its course. My own objective was to regain my freedom, and so, starting that night, I began to think in earnest of running away, although the notion of escape was still only an idea that had germinated like a seed in my mind—it grew as the days passed, but at the time I did not know how or to what place I might flee.

The right moment—the time to harvest the crop—came only when I received news that rocked me to the core, left me so dizzy I nearly fainted, as if a lightning bolt had come from the sky and struck me. I almost didn't believe what I heard from Mukhlis Farouq, that day at his bookshop. "Is this a joke, Mukhlis?" I asked him.

He glanced toward the door of the shop, and when he was sure there was no one there, he said, "How could I joke about such a thing?"

My heart nearly burst from my ribs. I clutched at my head to stop it exploding from the impact of the thing that had just landed on it. "Repeat what you just told me," I said.

"I can't believe it myself," he replied. "I still have my doubts, but the letter declares that Yusef 'lives— he is alive'."

My fingers shook, and my words tumbled out of my mouth. "Show me the letter," I said. "It could be that someone is playing a trick on us, taking advantage of our feelings."

He looked toward the shop entrance again, then drew a small sheet of paper from his pocket. I took it from him before he even held it out to me, and read, "Yusef has not been devoured by wolves. He lives— he is alive."

Merely this earthshaking phrase, which created no more than a tiny opening I had no idea how to probe.

"What are you telling me, Mukhlis? Who gave you this note?"

"I don't know who it was that stuck it in the door of the shop."

"Have you told anyone in his family?"

"Where would I find his family? Didn't you know they moved away somewhere?"

"I had no idea—this is a complete surprise. I stopped visiting them a long time ago, because of his mother's attitude toward me after I got married. Where did they go?"

"I don't know. They were fed up with the persecution, and it just wasn't possible for them to live here anymore, especially after his father's death."

"Try to find out where they are and let them know about this."

"Even if I knew where they were, I wouldn't want to plant a hope that might be false."

"Even false hope would be better than despair taking over their spirits. Besides, a moment ago you said he was alive. Living."

"I said that based on the words in the note—I, too, would like to plant a hope in my own soul, but I have to hold back, to avoid being too hasty in a matter so critical."

For days upon days, we waited for some further enlightenment that might come and expand that narrow opening. Back and forth we went, Mukhlis and I, trying to make sense of things. Hope would start to dwindle when it occurred to us that it might have been a bad joke someone had played for reasons of his own. Who, we wondered, would play such a nasty prank, who would make a game of something so serious? Then we would resume, our own hearts filling once more with hope, as we searched for a way to get at the heart of the truth. And we waited, in case perhaps a lantern might light up all at once and illuminate the darkness we were in.

We passed the days, one after another, Mukhlis and I, keeping what was on both our minds absolutely secret. We did not discuss it by telephone, knowing that the lines were tapped; rather, I would go to the little bookshop on the pretext of buying newspapers or some magazine or book. When there was a customer in the shop, I would pretend to occupy myself with looking over the books. Once the customer left, I would approach Mukhlis, who would raise his eyebrows and spread his hands, as if he had read the question in my eyes before it reached my lips:

"No news, but I haven't given up hope."

"Nor I, but be careful and make sure it's not a setup—they suspect anyone with ties to Yusef."

"They've made no secret of their suspicions, ever since the first interrogation."

"Why, in your view, after nearly a year, does this bit of information—suspect, so far—come along to alter the dormant flow of that river whose name is 'Absence'?"

"I have no answer to that. Maybe the information is accurate, but, until now, circumstances prevented whoever brought it from doing so. At any rate, everything will come to light in time."

There are embers in the heart that are never extinguished. A headache had settled into my skull, my sleep was disturbed, and the problems with my husband intensified. I would boil over for the most trivial reasons and would provoke him in order to vent my own burden of anger. When he recited his poems, I would tell him what I had not dared to say before: "Who was it that set you up by telling you you were a poet?" I was indifferent to whatever his reaction might be; I had deprived him of all the pleasant feelings any husband might hope to find in his wife, because with him I had no such feelings. I burst into tears any time Yusef's face came to mind and I imagined him coming back, learning of my marriage to Mu'nis, and shouting at me that he wished our separation had continued until his dying day. Maybe he would disappear all over again, swallowing the bitterness of defeat and shutting away his sorrow in the depths of his soul. But whatever state of mind he might be in, would he write off the woman he once loved—a woman called Narjis?

As for my husband, I had written him completely out of my life. I began to taunt him, drawing him more and more onto quarrelsome ground, toward critical junctures, to induce him to make the decision I had already made myself but not spoken aloud. If this didn't work, I was going to run away all the same, leaving him a note in which I would ask him to divorce me in absentia; if on the other hand I succeeded, and got him to fling in my face his declaration of divorce, I would write to him: "You have divorced me before God, and I hereby announce it publicly." Either way, he wouldn't want to become the butt of people's jokes. "Why did Narjis run away?" they would muse. "She must have a lover, and she's run off with him." Then he would hang his head before them, having lost all their respect; they would scorn him, subjecting him perhaps to wounding comments that impugned his manhood. Thus he would be compelled to announce that he had divorced me, after which it would be no concern of his just where I had gone, or why; nor would it occur to him that I had run away in order to find the man I loved, Yusef—he would find that implausible, Yusef's life having ended the moment he disappeared. For Mu'nis, life was for the living, not for the lost and gone. Mu'nis was a man who loved life, which he treated it as a comedy—although it was true that my being interrogated

a second time had had a sobering effect, the first interrogation having occurred before we were married.
He passed one black day, sweating and scared, for he
had dreamed of being one of those "poets of the mil-
lion," competitors to receive that sum from the president, who would award it when pleased by a poem
that praised him.

Two weeks had passed when Mukhlis placed a second slip of paper in my hand. "Meet Mohsin al-Alwan," it said, "after 4:00 p.m., in his office. He is the
one who can help you get to your friend."

"Who is Mohsin al-Alwan?" I asked Mukhlis.

"All I know," he replied, "is that he has an office for transcription and copying in Rashid Street.
I've visited him twice, as I recall—this was several
months ago—to photocopy a couple of books. He's
risking his life, obviously."

I looked at him, uneasy about this Mohsin al-Alwan. Making no secret of my suspicions, I said, "Who
says he's not working for the authorities?"

Mukhlis dismissed my concerns, saying, "No,
no—you're off the mark with that kind of thinking. Mohsin al-Alwan's office is nothing but a front
for other operations, including the photocopying of
banned books. He's a man who makes his living in
his own particular way, even if it's dangerous."

The first part of the thread was the note—it led
us to Mohsin al-Alwan, who told us that Yusef was
in one of the prisons at Khanaqin. When Mukhlis

inquired as to the source of his information, he evaded the question. "Rest assured," he told us, "that I'm telling you the truth. This is what I do, and I've never let anyone down." He could make arrangements for Mukhlis, or for someone in Yusef's family, to go there and find out the truth, if they wished. Mukhlis informed him that Yusef's family had moved away and we didn't know where. I made clear my own readiness to undertake the journey, and Mukhlis raised no objection—he knew that he was unable to take on this mission, not only because he sensed that he was watched and vulnerable, but because he was his family's sole breadwinner. He did not wish for his mother, his father, his wife, and his children to be cast adrift if he was gone. Also, he knew that I did not consider myself married, and that nothing I cherished was left to me but Yusef.

I shook the dust of fear from my heart, bearing a lamp with a tiny flame of hope on which I fixed my resolve—even if the hope was a mere slip of paper shoved under the door of a bookshop. And so I embarked on my journey, which would take me to what I sought, or would cast me into the unknown . . . and oh, that "unknown," in this country of mine.

4

His face was serene, although his features might alter in his rare moments of anger. His voice was deep and low and steady. He had eyes of brilliant green, as if God had consigned his lush forests to them. He was of towering height, handsome, vibrant and overflowing with love for life. This was Yusef, the young man who had disappeared in mysterious circumstances. In such a time as this, it was no wonder that anyone should disappear—a time of exile and of vanishings; of eternal sorrow, lost love, and strangled hopes; of mothers languishing in grief for their sons, sweethearts scorched by the embers of their love, and unmarried women whose dreams died because so many men had been killed in past wars, while so many others had sealed their hearts, knowing that wars in unending succession awaited them. It was a time in which the soldiers' helmets came off only when their owners died; a time in which one came to fear one's own imaginings, even the shadows of trees shading the house—for what these might conceal among their branches could expose whatever people in their unprotected homes were up to; a time to fear neighbors, family members, or slips of the tongue, or indiscretions whether committed on the telephone or picked up by the infinitesimally minute devices that were tucked into corners and inserted into mattresses, to detect every word, every sound.

As a tactic to stop Yusef's family from pursuing their inquiries about him, to put an end to this talk so displeasing to those running the country, his father was summoned one day to the party headquarters, where the chief officer said something to him that nearly knocked the breath out of him. "Stop your lying," he was told. "You know where your son has run off to. We've ascertained that he harbors dangerous ideas, and has fled to a rebel area to join the fifth column. We've gone easy on you up to now, since you're an old man, and not well, although we've wanted to keep you in our sights while you've got a head on your shoulders. Tell your wife to hold her tongue—she's spreading a lot of nonsense about in order to cover her son's tracks. If she doesn't, one day she'll find herself with no tongue to hold."

This incident was directly responsible for the death of Yusef's father a few days after he answered the summons.

"They planted terror in Yusef's father's mind," said Mukhlis Farouq to Narjis, "so that he would quit asking about his son. And they know that Yusef didn't run away; indeed they know very well that they are the ones who made him disappear, but this is their way of obfuscating their crimes."

"What did Yusef do," asked Narjis, "to make them go after him? Was he affiliated with some proscribed party without my knowing it?"

Mukhlis swore to her that Yusef had no connection to any forbidden group. "It was just that he was sometimes, at the coffeehouse, too bold in expressing his opinions on the national politics that had brought disaster on our heads. Maybe one of them was recording what he said—or else the place was bugged."

"What was he saying?"

"He didn't say anything that should have led to this sort of disappearance. He talked about the sufferings of people who had lost their means of subsistence in the marketplace, and the monopolies held by those who could control commodities. He talked about the militarization of our lives, and the general lack of freedom to dissent. I think, though, that it may have been the last time—when I wasn't there—that did it. Some days after he disappeared, I heard from someone who'd been present that day that at first the conversation was about literature. One of the people who were there had brought along a copy of the novel *The President*, and the title made someone else uneasy, because he thought the reference was to our own president. He looked askance at the book, but its owner dispelled his doubts by clarifying things: The novel is by the Guatemalan writer, Miguel Angel Asturias, and it's about the authoritarian government of the dictator, Cabrera, who ruled Guatemala with fire and the sword, and took pleasure in killing his own people.

"From there the conversation really took off. So as to avoid going in a direction that was forbidden, this person told a joke to the group. It was something that happened in one of the rooms at the Ministry of Culture, when the novel fetched up with a censor. Before this censor realized what was in the book, he got carried away, and shouted at one of the officials, a woman called Hasna, 'What kind of idiot writes "Mr. President," without appending, "May God protect and preserve him"?' Then he handed the book to the official, having written on a paper he taped to the book jacket, 'Reprint the cover with the words "May God protect and preserve him" added.' The group laughed.

"Except for Yusef—he didn't laugh. Instead he said, 'I've read this novel before, and it's truly applicable to our wretched situation. It's as if Asturias had lived in Iraq, or was one of us, witnessing and connecting with the authoritarianism under whose yoke we live.' No one made any comment. They rubbed their necks, then one by one they slunk out of the coffeehouse. Then—speaking to the last of them, who was just about to leave—Yusef said, his tone laced with sarcasm, 'Cowards. The likes of you are the reason for the state we're in.'

"One of them must have reported him."

With Yusef's disappearance, his friend Mukhlis Farouq's habitual smile likewise vanished, especially after he himself was arrested, two weeks later, and subjected to a humiliating interrogation, despite the authorities' knowledge that he had not been with the group who had gathered at the coffeehouse on the day in question. When all trace of Yusef was lost, and despair began to settle into Narjis's heart, she did not sever contact with Mukhlis, for he was the only person in whom she could confide her secrets; he was also the one who might receive information about Yusef before it reached his other friends. So she kept in touch with him, meeting him at his little bookshop on Mutanabbi Street. Perhaps, despite the anguish that pervaded her heart, she would hear some news that could stop the pain that was like a hemorrhage.

At this time she was rationing her visits to Yusef's family, because she sensed that she was being watched, as she, too, had been summoned to party headquarters and put through an interrogation from which she emerged terrified, transformed into a bundle of nerves. Then came her marriage, which distanced her from them for good. Yusef's mother no longer felt comfortable seeing her, and told her so in no uncertain terms—indeed, unkindly: "What business have you got with us? Go back to your husband—leave us alone." Narjis was about to try to explain why she had married, but the mother silenced her with a sharp look, which held no sympathy. "Quiet! I won't listen to lies. You're no longer welcome in my house."

Any time Narjis was alone, she was seized by memories calling her back to the time of her early

innocence, when she and Yusef were children playing together. How her mother had scolded her: "Girls
play with girls—if your father knew, he'd keep you
out of school."

"Yusef is nice to me, Mama."

"He's still a boy, child."

"I know, Mama—did I say he was a girl?"

"Don't you talk back to me like that, or I'll lock
you up! Get on with your schoolwork—have you
done your assignments for class?"

"I did them, Mama—check my notebooks to
make sure."

Yusef appeared, approaching from behind her
mother as she was bent over the notebooks, his hand
over his mouth to keep from making any noise. He
gave Narjis a signal, by which she knew that he would
wait for her on the riverbank, where she would join
him when he went fishing. She would hand him the
bait for the hook, and he would cast the line, and
then she would sit next to him and wait for a fish to
take the bait. Or they might collaborate in construct-
ing houses made from the golden sand. Each time the
river washed them away, the children rebuilt them.
Sometimes he would fashion a many-winged bird
for her out of clay and say to her, laughing, "If your
mother locks you up, just climb onto this bird and
come to the river, so we can play."

For years, even after her mother died, her eyes
would pursue Narjis, along with her remonstrances

as she followed her every move, demanding of her daughter whenever she was about to leave the house, "Where are you going, Narjis?"

5

It was a little after midday, and the car was parked at a repair shop on an unfenced lot. Fatigue showed in all their faces. Narjis looked around her—this, then, was Khanaqin. Then she wanted to make sure, so she turned to the older woman. "Yes, this is Khanaqin," the woman told Narjis, without turning toward her; Narjis, for her part, had her eyes fixed on the short man, who glanced quickly in their direction, then walked between the cars on the lot, followed by the two women. It had not occurred to Narjis that, when she followed the short man, the older woman would do likewise; she had thought they would part ways as soon as they left the repair shop, for their purposes in being here were different—or so she believed.

As they all left the shop, they were plunged into the commotion of the market: little carts bearing vegetables, the voices of the vendors continuously calling out to attract buyers, porters who never took their eyes off the customers, and all the hue and cry in a language incomprehensible to the women who had come from the capital. It was an extensive market, laid out parallel to a piece of elevated ground, and interspersed with houses, ancient structures, and stores selling everything from handmade carpets to handbags of fabric or leather, as well as suitcases, belts, socks, Kurdish-style slip-on shoes known as *gaiwa*, plastic kitchen utensils, aluminum cooking pots, inexpensive trinkets, narghiles, tobacco, various kinds of locally made soap, nuts, raw honey, cheeses, dates, strings of dried figs, sweets, and ready-to-wear clothing smuggled from Iran.

What most astonished Narjis, however, was that the older woman carried on walking beside her, following the short man—the driver beside him—each time he turned this way or that, even when he entered a narrow alleyway. This was flanked on both sides by old stone houses. Conspicuous on the right-hand side, about halfway down, was a small coffeehouse in which old men dressed in colorful trousers were gathered, smoking, drinking tea, and playing dominoes. The driver made for the coffeehouse, saying to the short man, "I'll wait for you here."

Neither of the women said a word. The alleyway angled to the left, into a section that seemed shorter than what they'd left behind; they could all see that it had no opening at the other end, but culminated in an old wooden door, on which appeared conspicuous drawings of flowers and leaves. In the center was a brass knocker, yellow with corrosion. The short man stood at the threshold, grasped the knocker and gave it three regularly spaced raps, then another three, after which a key turned, a bolt slid, and the door was opened by a man in his mid-fifties. He was tall, and of light complexion, with wide green eyes. Immediately upon seeing the short man, he exclaimed, "Abu Asim? Welcome!" And with that he ushered them all inside.

Are you, Narjis, entering heaven or hell? Have you escaped the broken-down car only to fetch up in a predicament that will lead who-knows-where? There was no time to react—the older woman, when Narjis turned to her, had already moved ahead, untroubled by any anxiety. So Narjis found herself entering the house as if an invisible hand had forcibly propelled her.

Upon stepping over the threshold into the house, the two women found themselves face-to-face with a woman in her late forties, who had emerged from one of the doorways. She had a very light complexion that showed a hint of pink, and wide eyes with thick lashes almost like an umbrella shading her blue-black irises. Her hair was parted in front and braided in two long plaits hanging to her waist. Although a little plump, she was well-proportioned. She wore a long, voluminous caftan in bright colors with turquoise-green dominant among them. Under this were wide trousers of the same fabric, and a sleeveless vest with embroidered edges.

The short man spoke with her in Kurdish, then turned and shifted his glance between Narjis and the older woman, introducing them to their hosts.

"Keke Mahmoud owns this house, and Madame Mizgin is his wife—they are among my dearest friends, and they offer splendid hospitality."

"Our home is blessed with women!" said Mizgin, welcoming Narjis and her companion. This was a Kurdish proverb, exalting the value of women in a household.

Turning to the short man, Keke Mahmoud said, "Friend, every time I see you, you're shorter than the last time! One of these days when I see you I'm going to think you're a lost child, looking for his mother!"

Abu Asim laughed. "And you're taller than ever," he said, "like a utility pole!"

"Unlike the government's utility poles, though, I'm not out of service." He guffawed.

Mizgin gestured to the two women to enter the guest quarters, but before they could make a move, the short man addressed them. "God willing, you'll find what you're looking for. And now, I must go."

"Where to?" Keke Mahmoud objected. "You've got to have lunch."

But Abu Asim excused himself. "I have many things to do," he said, "and the driver is waiting for me. I'm going to Kwisanjaq on another errand."

"Wait a moment, then," said Keke Mahmoud. "I have a gift for you." He went into another room.

Narjis, meanwhile, turned to the short man. "When will you return, Abu Asim?" she asked him.

With a slight smile he replied, "At this point my part is concluded. Someone else will come and take over from here."

Mizgin handed him a bowl of kefir, and he drank it while waiting for Keke Mahmoud to return. He reappeared, carrying a nylon bag, from which he drew a pair of *gaiwa*. "These are my own handiwork, as you know," he said, "and I fashioned the heel of this pair expressly for you."

Receiving the shoes, clearly as delighted as a child, Abu Asim thanked Keke Mahmoud, then turned to the rest of the group. "God be with you," he said.

As he prepared to take his leave, Keke Mahmoud said to him, "Be careful. If they catch you, they won't hang you by a rope."

Abu Asim paused, and looked at Keke Mahmoud, perplexed. "What do you mean, Keke?" he said.

Laughing, Keke Mahmoud replied, "What I mean is that they won't be able to find your neck to put a noose around it, so they'll have to shoot you!"

"Better that than death by nitric acid."[1]

Mizgin conducted her two guests to an iron door at the end of a corridor. She pushed it and it opened into a little house that was annexed to the main building.

1. Death by nitric acid: a method of torture and execution, involving the placement of victims in this chemical, which would kill them slowly.

It contained only the guest area, a bathroom, and a little square courtyard. The courtyard was open to the sky above, with a very healthy fig tree in the middle of it. Then there was the guest area, beginning with a long and spacious room on the right-hand side. Opening onto the courtyard and taking up half of a wall there was a single window, hung from the top of which was a thick curtain featuring red and purple stripes. The floor was laid with a carpet of the local variety, with its distinctive designs in many brilliant colors, red dominant among them. Resting on the carpet, at the base of the walls, were colorful woolen cushions. A picture hung upon the wall opposite the window, framed in beechwood and depicting trouser-clad men, young and old, some carrying rifles and wearing ammunition belts, and positioning themselves behind rocks, while others stood near a tree or sat at the foot of a mountain. In the middle of another wall was an image, on paper, of a forest dense with trees; this picture was partially hidden behind a long table, on which was a large dish filled with various kinds of nuts and seeds—walnuts, hazelnuts, watermelon seeds, almonds, pistachios, and cashews.

Mizgin reached for the switch to the ceiling fan and turned it on. When Narjis and the older woman had seated themselves on the woolen carpet, Mizgin excused herself and left the room. Narjis looked at her companion with a question in her eyes. She wanted to say, "Why did you lie to me? Why did you say you were coming to Khanaqin to visit your sister?"

The woman understood the look Narjis gave her. "It appears," she said, "that we are in the same predicament. You're well aware that what we're doing has to be kept secret—and you and I don't know each other."

"That's true." Shaking her head, Narjis added, "May God free us of our anguish . . . what should I call you?"

"Umm Hani. And you are?"

"Narjis. Will we be staying long in this house, Umm Hani?"

"I don't know. I've spent so much of my life waiting to pass from one thing to the next that I've got used to it."

Mizgin returned carrying a tray which held a teapot and glasses, as well as dishes of white cheese, curdled milk, and loaves of bread. In her halting Arabic, she reiterated expressions of welcome, repeating the Kurdish proverb, "Our home is blessed with women!" The aroma of the tea as it pervaded their exhausted bodies gave Narjis a sense of languor, but she could not stand her own body, for she had been sweating profusely throughout the journey, so she asked Mizgin whether she might bathe. While she took some clean clothing and a towel from her bag, Umm Hani lifted her dress, and unfastened a back-brace she had been wearing. Taking a deep breath, she said, "This brace helps relieve fatigue—I suffer from back pain."

"May God heal you," said Narjis.

There were long hours ahead of them, and the wellsprings of the soul were full to overflowing.

6

In Baghdad, the day was still veiled in dust as the call to noontime prayer issued from loudspeakers. It was Friday. Mu'nis al-Shaa'ir, waking, tossed and turned, trying to go back to sleep. Having failed, he got out of bed and made his way to the bathroom to wash his face. At this time each day Narjis, aggrieved as always, would have begun preparing lunch. It was her habit, when she washed the dishes, or when she either took something from its place or put it back, to make a racket, as a means of giving vent to her un-happiness, without a care for the effect of the noise on her husband, who came home drunk each night. He would fall into a stupor, while Narjis would carry on a protracted struggle in the room upstairs to snatch a bit of time for sleep, often waking him with whatever she was doing, until, early in the morning, she got up. Sometimes he shouted from his bed, calling to her, but she didn't respond as she had used to do in the days before he swore the oath to divorce her. Now she had achieved her goal, and matters between them were finished as far as she was concerned. All she had left was her noisemaking—she was willing to break anything just to give herself a sense of relief, to do things she had never done before just to disrupt the course of her fate, whether it was to smash dishes or have the television on at top volume.

But on this day it was different. Mu'nis noted the absolute stillness of the house—it was not like Narjis to sleep this late. He came out of the bathroom and stood at the bottom of the stairs. "Narjis," he called. "Narjis! Narjis!" But he did not hear her voice in reply. "Could it be," he wondered, "that she's done something to herself? Has she committed suicide?" This was what occurred to him, for she had uttered the word "suicide" in his hearing more than once, and things had been bad between them the previous night, before he went out on the town. So he climbed the stairs to the room at the top to look for her, but didn't find her there. He went back downstairs, thinking she might have gone to the market to buy some supplies. He went into the kitchen and made tea for himself. He took three pieces of Kiri cheese from the refrigerator and a loaf of bread, placed the food on a tray, and brought it to the table in the adjacent room, where he set it down near the candy dish. Spying a slip of paper folded inside the dish, he took it and read, "You have divorced me before God, and I am publicly declaring our divorce. You will not see me again."

Stunned, he sat for some minutes without moving. Then he flew into a rage, like a mad bull. He threw the tray of food to the floor and pounded the candy dish with his fist, scattering colored sweets in all directions and shattering the glass. He burst back into the kitchen, where he grabbed all the dishes and kitchen implements from their places and flung them down, breaking them on the tiles. Leaving the kitchen with a knife in his hand, he ascended once more to the upstairs room. He opened Narjis's closet, pulled out all the garments she had left behind, and proceeded to tear into them as if he was chopping up her body, avenging his injured honor. Having done all this, he went downstairs again, drained of strength, sat down in the living room, and wept like a woman just bereaved of her newborn child.

He was still in tears when he heard the doorbell. He looked out the window and saw his mother. Hurrying to the bathroom, he washed and dried his face. Then he opened the door. His mother was carrying a bag of vegetables, but when she went to put it in the kitchen the mess in there took her aback. "Mu'nis," she exclaimed, "what is all this?"

She turned to find Mu'nis behind her, with an expression on his face that failed to conceal his misery—indeed, he was unable to hold back his tears, which flowed once again. Dismayed, his mother beat her breast and cried, "What has happened, son? Speak to me!"

The note was crumpled in his fist—he handed it to her, so that she could read it for herself. She did so, then shouted at him again. "And here you are, crying like a woman? Why did you divorce her, then?"

He wanted to tell her about how Narjis had been behaving toward him in these latter days, but she silenced him with a wave of her hand, and asked him where Narjis might be found, so that she could go and effect a reconciliation between them. Mu'nis said he didn't know, and that, even if he had known, it was too late. In the silence that fell between them, they bowed their heads. Then she looked up. "In that case," she said, "you'd better save face by making a public announcement of the divorce. Otherwise, we'll be everyone's laughingstock."

7

The vault of the sky opened out over the roof, which was paved with brick and edged with stone. The stars appeared at an immense distance, farther away than impossible dreams, with the moon guarding the night, solitary in its place, aloof from God's earthbound creatures. To the side of the roof Mizgin arranged places for sleeping, for the guest quarters were hot even with the ceiling fan running. She laid out a mat and spread carpets over it, on which she placed foam mattresses and colorful pillows.

Mizgin wished her guests a comfortable night, but there was no rest for the two weary bodies, and their eyes refused to close. Dinner had been finished a half-hour earlier, a Kurdish dish known as *doina*. This was made from crushed wheat mixed with yogurt and onions pan-fried in hot oil, and seasoned with spices. More than half the food had been left on the plates, road fatigue combined with fear having robbed the two women of appetite. Silence prevailed for a while, the women gazing toward the stars, not for the pleasure of their twinkling light, but as a kind of summoning of their faraway hopes, resting perhaps in the stars' illumination.

A tiny opening for conversation was initiated by Umm Hani, who shifted her position to turn toward Narjis. "Have you lost a loved one," she asked, "—someone for whom you're searching now, as I am?"

Narjis felt as if she needed to unknot her tongue, and let Umm Hani hear her story, since they were united in the trouble that had brought them both to his place. So she bestirred herself and turned to her companion. "Yes," she said, but she didn't wish to be the first to tell her tale, and so she gave the question back. "Who is the loved one you've lost?"

"Ah," said Umm Hani, with a sigh that seemed to come from a deep cleft in her chest. "It's my son," she said.

The winking stars faded, as if Umm Hani's sigh had risen up to pass through them and dim their glimmering light, so that they also might attend to a new chapter in the collection of stories belonging to women flayed by sorrow.

8

"No one bids them 'Good morning,' they can't hear the sparrows chirping or the doves cooing or the rooster crowing to announce the sunrise. No one comes to visit them there, nor do any of them leave that place.

"Who are they, and what place is it? In what direction relative to Baghdad? Why are they prevented from seeing the sky? And how has a patch of the earth come to enclose them, so that they live outside of time, not knowing how much of their lives has passed, or how much remains?

"They are the living dead, or the dead who yet live—it's all the same. Strangers, cut off from their families, and yet at the same time not far away; wretched ones, forsaken by all that is sacred, bearers of sin who have committed no sin; the lost and forgotten who will have no graves to commemorate them when their time comes—and indeed, who in the end will even say that they have died? Such are the questions in mothers' hearts. Perhaps the loved ones they bore and raised are made to die to spare the expense of food and medicine, restoring their honor and dignity, however fragile. That would be better for them, says whoever has jurisdiction over their souls: They're going to die sooner or later, so why not have mercy on them and hasten their end?

"The building is older than any of the soldiers guarding it—much older, its age apparent in every one of its corners. Hundreds have entered it since its establishment in the early 1950s, and for many years its beds have been occupied by invalids, exhausted bodies crowding the place more and more from one day to the next, emerging only to return to their Creator; or if one did come out alive, then it must mean that a miracle had visited him, and he had recovered.

"This was in a previous era—that of a disease known for passing through the air and infecting the healthy, a calamity that spread from time to time in the poorer quarters. People would rush the invalid to that building, along with prayers that he might recover and return to his family. At the time there were no guards furtively standing watch over the place— for many years it remained like any other hospital, with nothing to distinguish it except that it was specifically for those suffering from tuberculosis. And now? What is this soldier doing, his weapon drawn, standing at the door of a hospital for tuberculosis patients?

"Times change. The scourge of tuberculosis receded from the land, making way for a different kind of illness, more virulent and more lethal—an illness not merely of the body, but, when it digs in deep enough, of the soul as well. There is no consolation for them—they are the untouchables, forbidden to see their families, cut off, their world contracted and narrowed, closing in on them until hope itself is a thing that becomes the single desire of every one of them.

"An utterly closed world, in a place where each day, until the end of their days, repeats itself as one in an almanac of sorrows. How can they come out? And how might they live their lives with their vision so diminished as to crush their hearts? These are the people afflicted with AIDS, first sequestered in this building during the late 1980s, and no one outside those walls believes that they are the victims of a drug imported by the government—a medicine that was contaminated with this accursed plague. And even if people were to believe it, they would pay no attention to anything but what they'd heard in the first place, to the effect that the cause of the disease was unnatural sexual relations. The moment anyone mentions the disease to them, they exclaim, 'God preserve me—those sons of the Devil, they should be killed!' In this way people rationalize killing them. Why, then, should they come out and die in the open, beset by curses and abuse? God alone knows them, and they await his mercy: the mercy of a God-given death, not death at human hands."

Umm Hani, pierced to the heart, told her story, which emerged along with her heart's blood. She swallowed, though her throat was dry, and said,

"They incarcerated two of my sons. They were receiving treatment for an inherited condition—hemophilia—and it turned out the medication that had been brought specially from France was contaminated with HIV. So the disease entered the bodies of everyone to whom the medication was administered—men, women, and children. They detained the families of all the patients and subjected them to testing. In some cases, family members themselves had caught the disease, and so they were confined as well. In the event that one of the patients died, the family was forced to sign a document stating that the death was from some other cause. This was so that the French company could be absolved of its responsibility, in exchange for a contract with France for weapons our government urgently needed for its war with Iran. As for the bodies of the dead, they were not turned over to the families. They were burned and buried in the desert."

Umm Hani swallowed again, and then continued. "I thought my two boys were still alive, as the years passed by. But after desperate efforts, and bribes paid to one of the guards, I learned that both my sons died a year after they were detained. I was provided with a copy of the death certificate, which did not mention that they had died of AIDS but cited a different disease. At the bottom of the document was the signature of my husband, who had never received any summons. Not long afterward, my husband died of cancer, and his body was held for several days, in order to ascertain, so I was told, the cause of death, to make sure that he hadn't died from something other than cancer—AIDS, in other words. After his death, raids on our house persisted, always on some pretext or other. They insisted I keep quiet, and forget the two sons I had had and lost, but I did not keep quiet. It became my mission, exclusively, to discover the whereabouts of my sons' bodies—but in what desert might I find them? I don't know—should I dig up the country's deserts in all their vastness, in hopes of happening upon them?"

Her furrowed brow contracted in dark lines, each of which told of a death deferred. Narjis poured water for her into a brass cup, from a pitcher Mizgin had left close at hand for them.

After she had drunk a little water, Narjis asked her, "Which boy are you looking for, then?"

Umm Hani said, choking on the words, "I'm looking for my third son, Namir, apple of my eye and the last of the fruit I bore. He was fifteen when his brothers were detained. He didn't have AIDS; he lived between fear and want . . . and the raids. Then, when he turned eighteen, he was drafted into the military and sent to the far north, so he decided to desert. I tried to dissuade him, but he was adamant. He confided in me, telling me that he was running away because the regime's wars would stop at nothing. He said he was tired of that life, and if he didn't run away then he would kill himself. I was afraid for him. I said to him, 'If they catch you, they will show you no mercy.' But he reassured me, saying that he would go to Turkey. He didn't tell me in which city he would be. All I know is the name of his Kurdish friend, Kouran Delshad Bakhtiar. I etched the name into my memory and wrote it on a slip of paper, so that it wouldn't be lost.

"I did not come across my son, and no news of him reached me. I don't know in what place he may have lived or died, and I haven't stopped searching, despite the tightened constraints on my movements. I pretended many times to be insane, until they believed it—this so that they would relax their terrible surveillance. I've traversed many of the northern cities of Sulaymaniyah, Irbil, Duhok, and Kirkuk; I've walked rugged roads, passed through villages mountainous and coastal, in search of the Kurd Kouran Delshad Bakhtiar, but I found no trace of him, as if he was no more than the name of a man not yet created. There were those who mocked me, and those who sympathized with my misfortune. They said I was looking for a needle in a haystack, but that doesn't trouble me—I would search every haystack to find out whether my son is alive or dead. If he is alive, I'll see him, and if he is dead, then I will die, and meet him in the presence of God.

"At last someone came along who let me know that I should travel to Khanaqin. I had been here four months earlier to visit the shrine of the blessed saint Khidr Ilyas, for I had been told that he was well-known for his miracles, and that if I visited all of his holy sites, I would find out where my son was. So I visited the sites in Baghdad, in Basra, in Diwaniyyah, Muthanna, Maysan, and Khanaqin. I placed candles for him on pieces of palm bark, set them afloat, and the water took them and they did not go out. This is what filled me with hope that my son was still alive."

Umm Hani fell silent, not because she had run out of words, but to dampen the burning flame that had flared in her heart after being kept for so long smoldering in ashes, and to take the deep breaths that would restore her equilibrium. Or perhaps there was a forgotten detail of her story that she had left unmentioned.

Narjis, straining toward her with every fiber of her being, was affected by her story. It was clear to Narjis that her own sufferings were more slight than she had thought, for knowledge of greater calamities diminishes our own.

The silence did not last long. Narjis asked Umm Hani, "Do you trust the information given to you by the person who directed you to come to Khanaqin?"

Umm Hani had been unable to suppress the tears she wanted to hold back. She drew a handkerchief from her pocket and dabbed at her eyes. "While I have two feet," she said, "and an unwavering resolve, I will chase even a mirage. A family member advised me to bide my time. She said to me, hoping to put an end to my mad search for Namir, 'If he were still alive after all these years, he would have come back to you by now.' I told her, as I was setting out on my journey,

'Then I will find out from Kouran Delshad Bakhtiar what happened to him, and I will go to where he is buried.'"

Narjis rephrased her question, thinking that perhaps whoever had directed Umm Hani to undertake this journey to Khanaqin was the very same person who had sent the tip about Yusef. "You haven't told me," she said, "where this directive came from."

"From a godly man who has lived among us for hundreds of years, but we don't see him—we sense him, rather."

This answer perplexed Narjis. When Narjis pressed her to explain, Umm Hani added, "From the blessed saint Khidr Ilyas."

At this point Narjis had the strong impression that this woman must be mentally unstable, and she felt her face soften into an expression of pity—but then Umm Hani removed all doubt. "My child," she said, "when no answer can be had from hard knowledge and we fall into despair, the spirits of the venerable saints catch us up and take us by the hand. This is what the saint, Khidr Ilyas, did. After I had toured his shrines and released hundreds of candles to the rivers' currents, to ensure that my prayers would reach him and in turn be delivered to God, he came to me in a vision. He said to me, 'Khanaqin will be your final journey. The border separating life from death is there.'"

Narjis did not care for Umm Hani's talk of "blessed saints" and her trust in them. God needed no intercessor for communion between him and the faithful. But she did not wish to disappoint this grieving mother, so she said only, "May God reward you in equal proportion to the patience of your quest."

The stars no longer gave off much light, as if they had retreated some distance; the moon, too, had withdrawn and was far away. It was past midnight, and Umm Hani stopped speaking. She was exhausted, for this story—the tale of her wanderings in search of some trace of her lost son—was one she had told hundreds of times, both to her familiars and to those whom she passed along the way, to the imams of mosques where she slept in strange cities, and to Bedouin sheikhs in the north, as she sought Kouran Delshad Bakhtiar. She had had her fill of weariness.

"And you?" she said now.

The question caught Narjis by surprise, as if it were a kind of barter she had not reckoned with. What could she say to this long-suffering woman, in the face of such woe? "I've come to look for my sweetheart, for whose sake I left my husband?" How could this woman comprehend her feelings, bereft as she was of three sons? What reply would she make? Her response might be a harsh one. Utterly confounded, Narjis turned over onto her back once more, facing the meager starlight. The answer she gave was likewise meager. "I lost my husband," she said.

Sometimes we lie not because we are liars by nature, but to ease our discomfort and avoid the disapproval of others. This was the approach Narjis chose, so that Umm Hani would not censure her, upon learning that she had left her husband for the sake of a man she loved, one she did not know whether she would ever see again, or whether he, too, would vanish into a haystack. Not the same thing, a lover and a husband, according to the traditions we have borne with for thousands of years.

To keep from confusing herself with more fibs, on top of the one she had found unavoidable when taken by surprise, she said, "I'll tell you the story another time—I feel tired just now. And you—mother who has fought so hard!—good night to you."

"Good night to you as well, my child."

But Narjis didn't sleep. In the quiet night her imagination was actively working on an improvised story of the loss of her husband, for she would be compelled to answer Umm Hani's question, should it be repeated. This was assuming no contingency should arise that would interfere with her staying in this house. She was despondent, not trusting the good intentions of the person who had arranged her journey. Perhaps she was the bait for a trap that would take her in a different direction and end up sending her back to Baghdad—not to the streets, the community, and everyday life, but to slow death in the gloomy chambers overseen by those devils. This prospect frightened her badly, but whenever she lapsed into despair, she was borne up again by a tremendous strength, and each time she was once more set to rights. It was never long, though, before the sense of well-being left her, and she fell back into the cycle of anxiety. There was nothing for her to do now but to devise her story.

In the dark of night were animated images, which descended upon her with the faint twinkling of the stars: "They took him, one morning, from the department in which he worked. They told him, 'You'll be back after just a few minutes; the matter in hand doesn't concern you—it's about someone else.' But there, at police headquarters, minutes turned into hours upon hours, then days upon days, with brutality and terror and torture, all unremitting. All this because he was the friend of a coworker who had fled the country and was connected to the resistance. They didn't allow me to see him. And then they took him to some unknown place, and since then he has not returned. This is my story—there's nothing new about it: a familiar tale that's been told again and again for decades. Hundreds have disappeared in the same way." She would go into no more detail than that—she would say that she didn't know very much, and therefore she had come here.

9

The morning of a new day: what would it bring? The first morning in a northern city, waiting for another man, who would pick up where the short man, Abu Asim, had left off. There were movements in the open space of the courtyard, flocks of sparrows emerging from the depths of the fig tree. There was a cockcrow, and the fragrance of plants scenting the air. Distant voices, carried off by the wind. A new day—and was there anything new?

Keke Mahmoud was getting ready to leave for his shop at the city market, where he produced *gaiwa*. The *gaiwa* is a type of traditional shoe, made by hand from the finest white cotton thread, affixed to a sole of cow's leather with colorful cotton stitching. This kind of shoe is suitable to northern climes in countries where there is such rugged ground and so many mountains they can't be climbed in ordinary shoes. His wife Mizgin helped him but did her work at home.

Umm Hani folded up her carpet and brought it down with her to the guest quarters, where she laid it in one of the corners, performed her ablutions, and prayed. Then she sat down to work her prayer beads and recite her supplications. Narjis awoke after that, picked up her own carpet, and went down. She greeted Umm Hani, and told her she had slept uneasily. Then she made her way to the bathroom to wash her face. When she returned, Mizgin had entered through the iron door. She greeted her guests. She was carrying a tray, on which was a large bowl of curdled cheese, honey in a small jar, a pot of tea, cups, and loaves of bread. A little while later, the women heard Keke Mahmoud clear his throat, announcing his presence. Mizgin said he wanted to say good morning to them before he left for work. Keke Mahmoud entered and greeted the guests, then said reassuringly, "All is well—we're waiting for Keke Tariq." Neither of them asked who Keke Tariq was—they knew that the reference was to the new guide, and they were sure that he would come . . . but when?

In the interval before Keke Tariq's arrival—an interval heavy with anticipation—stories were told, whose details, now laid bare, Narjis would not have known if it had not been for this journey, the outcome of which she could not predict. If it should conclude without her finding Yusef—and it was this outcome that would most distress her—would she return to Baghdad? And what would she do there? How many would cast stones at her, thinking themselves without sin? And what if she should be subjected to interrogation by government agents—interrogation and violation? Or would it be better to stay hidden in Khanaqin, seeking a different life there? Was this a safe place for her, when the eyes of the authorities pursued even ghosts along tortuous roads and into mountain caves? And who were these people who worked to find those who had disappeared? To what end did they do this work, and what was in it for them? Who was Mohsin al-Alwan, to begin with, and who were Abu Asim, Keke Mahmoud, Keke Tariq? It was all, in those moments, a mystery to her, incomprehensible. Ah, Narjis, such an unsettling time, nothing foreseeable with any certainty.

Affirming her husband's words, Mizgin said, "Rest easy—Keke Tariq will come. It's just that it's the need for him to move in safety that determines when he can get here. He knows his work well. I'm going to market now to buy vegetables. If a knock comes on the door, don't answer it. My husband, Mahmoud, won't be back until the end of the day."

Who would knock on the door? No one. It was just a precaution on Mizgin's part, addressed to two women whom she didn't yet know. Time was oppressive, with the door to the unknown still locked and beyond reach. Narjis was alert for the question to which Umm Hani would doubtless return, regarding Yusef's disappearance. She sat, thinking fretfully how to get the question out of Umm Hani's mind, or at least defer it. "What do you do," she said, "when you fall into a well of hopelessness over your repeated attempts to learn the fate of your son?"

As if she had dealt with this kind of question a thousand times already, Umm Hani replied without hesitation, "If there were any place in my heart for hopelessness, we would not have met on this mission, my girl. I am made of resolute endurance, and the calamities I have suffered did not bring me down. Otherwise I would have been laid in the earth a long time ago. You are still young and unschooled in life's brutal tribulations. You must comprehend them and prepare yourself against them, before they cast you down into despair."

"But no matter how much I've managed to assert my own will, my heart is still consumed with fear. How do I drive out the fear, my friend?"

"Let it take its own time," said Umm Hani, "and come to its own end. When we are afraid of something, we think about how to avoid it, and we can never put it out of our minds. So this is how I handled it. If I had been afraid of the authorities, for example, I would have cowered in my house, awaiting death, without knowing what had become of my sons. Do you think I am so very courageous? Not in the least. It takes a dose of courage and a dose of fear together to follow life's rules."

"But life's rules are unfair."

"They are fair—it's just that humans confound them."

"We are of an era whose very air is bloodstained."

"And what era *isn't* bloodstained? From the start of Creation, from the first crime in history, goodness

has been sacrificed to evil. Is there anything more
dreadful than the killing of a brother by his brother?
Qabil killed his brother Habil, and yet people name
their children after the killer, Qabil, while no one
calls his son Habil,[1] as if thrusting the goodness away
from themselves. What is painful in our case, child, is
that we have not found our loved ones, nor observed
the proper mourning for them. We don't know where
on earth they died or what piece of earth holds their
bodies."

"You seem sure of their having died, and that it is
corpses you are seeking."

"Nothing is absolutely certain. The guard who
delivered my son's death certificate could have forged
it, stolen the stamp, to put a seal on the document and
get rid of me once and for all as soon as he'd taken the
money. I believe that miracles still happen, and that
they occur only in their own time, but I assume the
worst outcomes, rather than fall prey to fantasy and
impotence. If my two older sons have in fact died,
then it is my duty to find my third son, as no one has
brought news of him to me so far."

"But still, my friend, I don't completely trust the
guides. Sometimes I'm overcome by feelings that
shake the hope within me, and I despair."

---

1. Qabil and Habil: Arabic names for Cain and Abel, re-
spectively; Qabil is the more common name in the Eastern part
of the Arab world, although neither name is common in Iraq.

"If you want to reach your goal, then cast those feelings of despair from your mind. For my part, I waste no time and spare no effort. Obstacles don't stop me."

In this way, between questions and answers, until Keke Tariq should come and until something should happen to alter the course of things, time passed. Mizgin returned from the market and came to look in on her guests, uttering no more than a few brief reassuring phrases. Then it was time for lunch. No Tariq had come knocking at the door.

Mizgin brought lunch—saffron rice with pieces of roast chicken, curdled milk, and a vegetable salad. Narjis's gaze hung upon Mizgin's features, in case they should disclose to her some reason for Keke Tariq's lateness. But Mizgin's determined smile disposed of reasons. "All in good time," her expression said, a notion repeated on her tongue, amid her brief sentences so frequently interspersed with Kurdish proverbs. She placed the food before her guests, and went out.

Umm Hani perceived Narjis's anxiety, her frustration with the passing hours. After they had eaten their lunch and drunk some hibiscus tea, Umm Hani said to her, "Develop the habit of patience, as I have done. I have waited; I've been placed by destiny face-to-face with death; I have seen what no one ever saw."

"What have you seen, Umm Hani?"

"I've seen horrors, child."

"Tell me about them. Maybe that will help make it easier for me to bear the difficulties I may encounter."

But before those "horrors" could form on Umm Hani's lips, she let out a long, deep breath—a sigh abruptly cut off, for they had heard three notes, which were followed by three more in the same pattern. This was something Abu Asim, previously, had done. It was as if the two women had been struck dumb. They stilled even the movement of their breath, their eyes trained upon the door of the guest quarters, awaiting any news from Mizgin, who did not take long to appear. "Grant her heart's ease, Lord of grace," said Umm Hani, as Mizgin entered and gestured to her, saying, "Keke Tariq is here. Madame, come with me."

Umm Hani rose quickly to her feet. Looking at Mizgin, Narjis said, "What about me?"

"Later."

Before leaving the guest quarters, Umm Hani went to Narjis and embraced her, expressing her hope that the door to peace of mind would open for her as well. Then the passing minutes weighed heavily on Narjis, her eyes fixed upon the door. She thought Umm Hani would return, but when she had waited a half-hour or so, impatient, crushed by the weight of time, she stood up and pressed herself to the window, facing the iron door behind which Mizgin and Umm Hani had disappeared. Then the lock turned, and the door opened. Mizgin entered with a glass of juice. Taking it from her hand, Narjis placed it on the table and turned to ask, "What news?"

Mizgin pushed one of her braids back behind her shoulder. "Your companion has left with Keke Tariq."

"What about me?"

"You must wait until he gets back. Keke Tariq won't go to two different places on the same errand."

"And when will he get back?"

"Once he's completed the first mission."

"But," said Narjis, "with all due respect, when will that be?"

"Forgive me—I don't know."

The time passed more slowly and more oppressively after Umm Hani's departure. Narjis did not know whether Umm Hani would come back to the house, or whether she had seen her for the last time, nothing remaining but a memory. Had Umm Hani really gone to a safe place? Or was it all a ruse, in which they came for those who were suspect on the pretext of offering assistance, only to cast them into the abyss? Narjis did not know, in these moments, on which shore she would alight: the one where she was at peace with herself, or the one where she was perpetually anxious and mistrustful of what was to come.

When dusk fell, and all was silence but for a few rustlings and wingbeats that reached her from among the branches of the fig tree, Narjis felt as though something was squeezing her heart. She felt as if she wanted to scream at the top of her lungs. With her hand pressed to her chest, she took a deep breath, resisting the scream, displacing it by remembering her time with Yusef.

The memories carried her far away, to the evening prayer, the time of their daily rendezvous on the terrasse, when the family was occupied with prayer. They would talk together hurriedly, promising to meet in another place, far from the families' rooftops and from the street and from people who knew them. Usually these meetings took place on the promenade at Zawraa Park, or else at Mukhlis Farouq's bookshop, Narjis having devised a thousand excuses to persuade her mother that she must be allowed to go out: a book she needed from the National Library or from Mutanabbi Street, or an ailing girlfriend she had to visit, or the father of one of her friends at school had died, and she must go and offer her condolences. If these and other pretexts forced her to put on a mask of sadness, shed tears, and wear a dark-colored garment, that was no problem—she was always clever at persuasion, deceiving her mother so that she could go and meet Yusef.

The memories emerged from their place, dropping like a gentle rain. She could almost hear his voice, his laughter, his breath; almost see the meadows of green in his eyes. Her waiting was like a night's downpour and the silence of the house as she crept up to the roof. She felt each word of love she had lived, every touch that had made her quiver. She returned to the sweetest of her memories, of the feeling that had burst forth on a particular evening. She had worn an amber-colored dress, figured with flowers like newly opened buds, stitched in purple. The fragrance of jasmine hung on the air, emanating from the garden of his house and stirring a desire for distant wanderings. His arms encircled her, and she rested her head on his chest. She could feel the heat of him and drink in his scent, sensations flowing through her whenever they touched. She wished she could fuse with him for the rest of her life. He pushed his fingers into her long hair black as night, and she was seized with rapture. No one could see them, for, as they clung together next to a wall, they found refuge in the shadows. The light of a distant moon pierced the darkness, and stole upon them, giving its blessing to their love.

Oh, for that heat, the passion when she was in his arms. His fingers would slip down from her hair and onto her neck, and her hands would move to draw his fingers away, to dampen the fire that set her body ablaze, but his hands—strong hands—would pull her toward him, and her eyes would gleam in the moonlight, with a luster that enticed him, drew his lips to hers. And there, beside the low wall that separated the two houses, which were joined at the back, they surrendered to their first kiss, the kiss whose taste would never leave Narjis's lips all the years of her life, however long. Just so, like a photographic image, the imprint of that kiss was hidden away in the depths of their souls: an image that challenged time to remain within the frame of incandescent emotions.

She closed her eyes to evoke that kiss—a kiss that was a mixture of arousal, rapture, confusion, and turmoil—in order to preserve its taste on her lips for as long as she could.

That night, as they drew back from the kiss, she was assailed by the dizziness of a love so intense it upset her balance. Her embarrassment before his gaze showing in her face, there was nothing for it but to escape, stumbling as she went. She descended two or three steps, before she sat down, gasping, to quiet her breath and restore the rhythm of her pulse. Then she went to her room and flung herself drunkenly upon the bed. She tried to sleep but could not; her body was still ablaze with passion, as if all her joints were infused with a feverish heat.

Now these sensations of love seemed to her a passing dream that had occurred that night, never to be repeated, or a brief cloudburst. Or it was as if it was all a figment of her imagination. As she wrapped herself in memories, she could not tell how the night passed, or when the memories ceased and the images fled, but she was fully aware that her love for Yusef, with all the reversals to which it had been subjected, was still the one thing that made her feel alive. For they had played together, and grown up, sharing their dreams as one. He would remain the love of her life, even after his disappearance and even should there come an end to all hope of his return.

Mizgin came with breakfast for her: clotted cream and honey with bread, and tea. Wishing her "Good morning," she placed the tray on the table, and said, "All will be well, God willing."

Thinking there might be news as to Keke Tariq's arrival, Narjis looked questioningly at her hostess. But Mizgin's next words disappointed her. "It may take some time, Madame Narjis, but all will be well. That is the nature of such difficulties: they come to a crisis, and then there is a resolution. Sometimes help comes within a day, sometimes several days. From north to south, this country is mined with government informants, so the work of the guides must be conducted in utmost secrecy. As our proverb has it, 'Do not approach the rabid dog.' This is what my husband Mahmoud wanted me to say to you. Have your breakfast, and be at ease, as if you were at home."

The little kitchen, its counters crowded with pots holding shade plants, opened onto a small back garden planted with flowers and shrubs. Mizgin, who stood in the kitchen washing vegetables, had served Narjis some *masto*, a combination of yogurt and salt, diluted with water. It was near noon, and Mizgin had asked Narjis to help her prepare lunch, rather than sit alone, consumed by her doubts. She set down a colander containing cilantro and chard she had just washed.

"Have you ever tried *tarkhina*?" she asked Narjis.

"No—I've never heard of it," Narjis replied.

"Well, *tarkhina* is made with wheat flour, to which you add powdered milk, cilantro, string beans, and chard—along with onions and spices, of course."

At this point Mizgin launched into her explanation as if she were teaching a class, talking about measurements and methods. Mizgin could see that Narjis did not understand everything she was telling her, preoccupied as she was, oppressed with waiting for she knew not what. From time to time, when Mizgin turned to her, smiling, Narjis returned the smile, but without knowing what had just been said to her. When she was on her own, she would pace the guest quarters, back and forth from the broad wall opposite the door to the window, and from the window to the door, then back to the wall again, then the window. There she would pause and cast her gaze over the courtyard, to the fig tree and its chattering birds, to the colorful butterflies that lit upon the flowers and drew out their nectar. She wished creation could be free of human beings, nothing remaining but the birds, the trees, and the butterflies, and gentle animals, for then it would be sweeter and kinder and more beautiful than this race of beings called "human," which made a mockery of nature and murdered its own kind.

When she tired of pacing to and fro, there was nothing left but to invoke her recollections of Yusef, to take herself back to those sublime moments, so as to ease the burden of the present, which sat so heavily upon her chest.

10

The forest was thick and deep, densely green with trees whose trunks were broad and strong. A dusty track cut through it; this was long and narrow, and appeared not to end where the picture ended. Time seemed to press upon Narjis's chest as if she lay crushed under the mountains, and there, all alone in the room, she studied the forest, depicted on paper, that was affixed to the wall, taking up the whole length of it. She entered into its minutiae. Her soul emptied out as she walked barefoot along this track, to the point where she could feel the dampness of the dirt beneath her feet, and gain a sense of peace by inhaling the fragrance of the plants. She would reach the end, to find Yusef waiting there for her, and then she would summon back with him those fleeting joys. She must visualize this, and bring about the miracle of their meeting, so as to deceive time, which did not advance. But the meeting did not go as she'd hoped, for she found him angry with her, his wrath nearly setting the forest alight. "You got married, Narjis? Why, then, have you come looking for me?"

But before she could justify what she had done by explaining the new circumstances that had arisen in her life after his disappearance, Mizgin called her back to the present. She hurried into the room, out of breath, and, seizing Narjis's hand firmly, urged her, "Quickly—you must hide."

"What's happened?"

"Don't be frightened—it's just a precautionary measure. Everything is secure here."

Mizgin moved the long table aside and took hold of the wooden frame of the picture of the forest. When she lifted it, a stone stairway appeared, which led downward. Nudging Narjis forward, she said, "Don't worry. We take every contingency into account."

The shadows engulfed Narjis, but Mizgin dispersed them, switching on the small flashlight she held in her hand. She gave this to Narjis. "Quick now, go downstairs," she urged. "Using this light to guide you, keep going until you reach the end of the tunnel. Sit down there and turn off the light. You mustn't come back until you hear my voice. If you're alarmed by noise in the tunnel coming from this direction, then you must go out by proceeding in the same direction you went. You'll find something that looks like a boulder, but it's not—it's cork, painted so that it resembles rock. Push it aside and go out. A few meters away you'll find someone who'll look after you." With that Mizgin left her, slipping the picture of the forest back into its place as she went.

Gripping the flashlight with trembling fingers, Narjis plunged into the tunnel that had been dug into the earth. Her breaths came rapidly, her heart seeming to swell as its rhythm accelerated. The air was dank, the place stiflingly humid and malodorous. She set her feet almost directly where the beam of the flashlight fell, conscious of her bare feet. She did not turn her head, and she had no sense of the distance she had to traverse; the tunnel seemed endless to her, and she felt off-balance—perhaps her blood pressure had risen or fallen. Fear caused her all at once to let the flashlight slip from her hand. The light went out, and complete darkness descended. She bent down and felt around for the flashlight, the stones on the ground cutting into her palms and the soles of her feet. Crawling forward, she searched until she found it, and grabbed hold of it like someone seizing a vial that held the elixir of life. Once more she illuminated her surroundings. She stepped on something damp, and heard a faint susurration, something like a squeak—it might have been the sound of a mouse. She hurried on as quickly as her feet could carry her. The tunnel wasn't long; it was fear that drew it out.

When she reached the end, she sat down on the ground. Taking hold of the object made of cork, she moved it slightly, to make sure it really wasn't an enormous rock that she'd be unable to budge. In vain, she tried to compose her breathing and her heartbeat. She extinguished the light, and the dimensions of the space were obscured. She was facing back in the

direction from which she had come, her mind beset by
evil thoughts. The house must have been subject to a
police raid, surely? What would happen if they knew
where she had gone? What fate would they devise
for her? What would she say if they arrested her and
dragged her off to their offices? "I'm looking for the
man I love"? They would mock her, of course, they
who didn't know the meaning of the word "love," or
what it meant for a woman to set off in search of a
man for whose disappearance they themselves were
responsible. They would say there must be something
else she had run away from when she violated the
prohibition that had been imposed upon her against
leaving the city. "This is a dangerous woman," they
would say, "—don't be fooled by her innocent face.
We'll flay her alive until she confesses."

She stayed crouched where she was, submitting
to the darkness and the way the time, seemingly arrested, squatted upon her chest. Her senses, though,
did not relax their vigil, but were alert to every noise,
even the sound of insects crawling, and from time to
time she still heard a faint squeaking, which now she
was certain was that of a mouse. Curling up in a ball,
she huddled in place, suspended in pitch-dark, and
closed her eyes against visions of ghosts, while her
mother's voice traveled through space to dispense its
reassurance: "There are no ghosts in the dark, Narjis." She quickly opened her eyes again, not because
of the voice that came to her from the next world,
but because everything was indistinct: There was in

this darkness no differentiation in color, nor could outlines be discerned in this corner or that; it was all one shade of pure black, an all-encompassing gloom, open to all manner of prognostications. The silence was loud, cacophonous with her rapid breathing and anxious heartbeat; time was not obedient to the hands of the clock—here time's scorpion-claws delivered their sting and injected their venom into the spirit before attacking the body. She could not cry out, and she could not see the ghosts with their glowing eyes, long noses, and tails of fire as she had seen them in her childhood; she feared, rather, the phantoms of living men that appeared before her— devils' spawn, coming from where she had entered. She stared into gaps in a darkness that had no gaps, entrenched, trembling, locked into her own silence as she struggled to suppress her terrors as best she could, as if these terrors were something palpable she could fend off with her hands, and if she could not do this then she must acclimate herself to them.

They say there's always a light at the end of the tunnel, so where was the light? When would it come and dispel the darkness? Where indeed was the end of the tunnel now? Was it the spot in which she now huddled, or in the direction she was facing—the way she had come? No light came, nor Mizgin's voice to rescue her. The minutes dragged on, stretching out idly, heedless of the woman who restrained her breathing as if the supply of air would soon be exhausted, while she prepared herself for some menace

that might beset her at any moment. She sensed something stirring on her right-hand side—a snake, perhaps. She shivered and cringed, bracing herself. Then
she felt a terrible chill, as if summer had given way,
with autumn following on its heels, come to freeze
her beyond endurance.

She thought about leaving, going outside. She tried
to shift the artificial rock, to see what was behind it
and who awaited her there, but when she stopped hearing the sound she thought was a snake, she drew back.
Perhaps it was terror that, in its extremity, had crept,
serpent-like, into all her joints, and she imagined it
as a snake. She must follow Mizgin's advice, and stay
quietly where she was, even though she no longer felt
quite certain of what Mizgin had told her, that all was
secure, every precaution having been taken.

What if the darkness never ended? What perils,
Narjis, might lie in wait for you then?

After an interval that felt to Narjis like an age and
delivered her up to all manner of terrors, Mizgin's
voice reached her like something coming from Sev-
enth Heaven: "Come on out, Madame Narjis." Her
throat dry and her face pale, she pressed the button
on the flashlight. She nearly lost her footing and fell
to the ground, so complete was the disorientation
that still possessed her. Fear had drained all her energy beyond the little required for her to stand up.
She went out into the light, ready to scream, but she
managed to regain her composure. She entered the

guest quarters like someone rising from the grave, and Mizgin replaced the forest that separated the room from the tomb.

"What happened, Madame Mizgin?" Narjis asked. "Didn't you tell me it was safe here?"

Offering Narjis a glass of water, Mizgin said, "The valley has its jackals—that is a Kurdish saying of ours—and so we are cautious, no matter how blessed we may be by peace."

Narjis drank half of the water, holding the glass in her still-trembling hand. "What peace, Mizgin?" she said. "I nearly had a heart attack. Tell me—did they search the house?"

Mizgin had brought along tools for weaving the fabric to complete one *gaiwa* shoe: white cotton threads interwoven with colored ones by clever fingers that knew where to insert the needle and how to draw the thread tight. Absorbed in her work, she said, "No, my dear, but there are those who cooperate with the authorities, even among the Kurds. Their own kith and kin don't matter to them—what interests them is what they can get by working for the regime. What happened an hour ago is that one of this type, Rayber, a cousin of ours, came to visit. Oh, if you knew this Rayber—he's like a snake hiding in your sock, he can't be trusted."

"Does he suspect you?"

"It's not unlikely, so caution is called for. He's true to his name."

"What does the name 'Rayber' mean?"

"'Leader and guide.' But what a difference, need-less to say, between him and the leaders and guides on the side of what is right and good."

"But you're cousins, you say?"

Mizgin's fingers paused at their work. She lifted her head and looked at Narjis. "That's not a reason for him to make an exception of us. If he could, he'd eat the honey and leave us to the bees, as the proverb says. He knows he is not welcome here, but he's boor-ish, a nag and a meddler. My husband Mahmoud told him, to prevent him from hanging about, that in a little while we were going to Jalawla to visit a friend who was ill, and that we wouldn't be back until late. Can you imagine what he said? "A party at Fati's house, while Fati is at Khati's!""

Amid the shadows of fear, a smile found its way to Narjis's lips. She asked Mizgin what the saying meant.

Taking her work into her clever hands once more, Mizgin explained without looking up, "It refers to when there is a guest in the house but the master of the house is absent." Then she stopped what she was doing, raised her head, and said, "The trouble is that the only place Rayber cares to sit is here, in this room, even though we have a guest room in the other part of the house."

"But couldn't you tell him you have a visitor who is female?"

"My dear, you don't understand. There are orders to inform the authorities who oversee these matters of any guests who stay longer than a week, and they would raise questions as to the reason for their visit, where they came from, and their home address."

"Why do you subject yourselves to the hassle of putting us up, Madame Mizgin?"

Narjis did not ask her what compensation they received in exchange for the risks they took, because they had yet to open any negotiations with her as to the price of her stay.

"This is a matter of conscience for us. We've seen affliction. Many of our family members died in the Anfal campaign.[1] When you know the calamities of others, your own troubles diminish. Imagine going home to your village, but not finding your family or any of the inhabitants of the village. All you see is corpses, everywhere: your father, your mother, your brothers and sisters, children, neighbors, even animals and birds—bodies swollen and distorted, strewn around the streets, the fields, the market-places, and inside the houses. My husband Mahmoud lost his entire family, while I lost my father, three of my brothers, my sister and her husband and children. I got pregnant twice, and gave birth to two baby girls, both disfigured because of the poison gas. I thanked God that they died within hours of being born, for they were frighteningly deformed. I had a hysterec-tomy to avoid any recurrence of such tragedy. To this day, survivors suffer from various kinds of cancer,

1. Saddam Hussein's genocidal campaign against Iraqi Kurds, in 1988.

and women give birth to children most of whom are deformed. What we do in order to try to help—well, it's a simple thing that may heal our wounds. There's no need for us to know everything in detail about a guest who takes refuge with us, so long as that guest has come by way of a trusted source. Rest easy, my sister, we know how to protect the innocent. You won't be here long—you'll find a solution to your problem, God willing."

"Does your husband know when Keke Tariq will come?" Narjis asked her then.

Mizgin's answer brought Narjis no relief from the urgency of her longing.

"He may come today," said Mizgin, "or tomorrow or after. That is out of our hands. Everything in due course."

She no longer looked at the dense, deep forest. Instinctively she avoided it, in case absorbing herself in its details might take her back to what lay behind it. It was enough to have lived that terrifying nightmare to which her own imagination had subjected her when she had undergone the actual ordeal, in all its particulars, of being in that place.

Likewise she gave up urgently questioning what was in store for her. She would let the days take their course however they might; if she did question them, she expected no answer. She had chosen an unknown path, and so it must be revealed to her with the passage of time—otherwise, why would we use the word "unknown"? If ill fortune should cause the revelation of things she did not like, she must be satisfied nevertheless, respecting the laws of the unknown and unknowable. Why should she rush the outcome? It might be that she would die before achieving her goal; or she might be subjected to the cruelest kinds of torture. Did she wish she had never left Baghdad?

Narjis had lost herself in these thoughts when her glance fell upon a ladybug, vivid in its red coloring and black spots, as the sunbeam coming through the window illuminated it. The ladybug was climbing the wall near the window, but it kept slipping and falling; no sooner did it pick itself up and start moving again than it fell once more, then got up again, only to repeat the pattern. Narjis felt something stir within her, a sense that she herself was the ladybug; the feeling overwhelmed her the fourth time the little creature fell, and at that moment she heard Mizgin's voice calling to her, "Come along, Madame Narjis—Keke Tariq is here."

With a gasp she got to her feet. Had she not held onto the wall she would have stumbled and fallen. Mizgin took her to the other part of the house. At last, after an age, Keke Tariq had arrived.

What awaits you, Narjis?

It was still early in the day. In the shade cast by an enormous oak tree sat Keke Mahmoud, and with him Keke Tariq, a man in his late forties, strongly built, with a piercing gaze. He wore brown trousers secured by a wide belt of embroidered cloth. Narjis greeted them as Mizgin went into the kitchen to make tea. Keke Mahmoud turned to Keke Tariq and, gesturing toward Narjis, said, "This is Madame Narjis." Keke Tariq greeted her; he did not need to ask what it was she wanted, for the knowledge had gone before her, as soon as she came to an agreement with Mohsin al-Alwan. He asked only for a document verifying her full name. She ran back to the guest quarters and fetched her identity card from her bag.

He scrutinized it with an eye well-rehearsed in these matters, then said, "I will take you to someone who has all the information about the disappeared in this region—there will be a price, of course, and . . ."

Narjis interrupted him. "I know, Keke Tariq—no need to be coy."

Keke Tariq smiled. "Madame Narjis," he said, accepting a cup of tea from Mizgin, "I don't take money. For me this is a matter of human responsibility. It is the other guide who has been assigned to your case who will take a fee."

She nearly wept. Another guide? So there was to be another torturous journey. But she said nothing, merely attending to Keke Tariq as he went on to say, "Initially you will pay him half the sum, with the other half to be paid only when you find the person you are looking for."

Mizgin handed her a nylon bag containing some food, as well as a pair of *gaiwa* shoes to help her on the trek, the uphill climb. With that she wished her a successful journey.

11

We left the houses, the marketplace, and the health clinic behind us. Keke Tariq carried for me the bag of food that Mizgin had prepared, while I carried my phantom hopes. Then we crossed an old stone bridge spanning a body of water that flowed sluggishly. "This," said Keke Tariq, "is the al-Wand River, which divides Khanaqin into two halves. This bridge, which is named after it and built from imperial brick, dates from the first half of the nineteenth century, the time of the Ottomans."

"Hmm," I said, unable to think of anything else to say, for what concern of mine was the bridge or who built it? I wasn't the one bisected by bridges, was I?

At the end of the bridge a youth in his twenties was waiting for us. "This is my nephew Sirwan," Keke Tariq told me as we got into the car.

"Hello," I said.

Sirwan drove for more than an hour. At a certain point, near a small shop displaying the name "Hama Houshyar's Shop," the car pulled up, and we got out.

Keke Tariq said, "We will use Hama Houshyar's telephone to set our appointment."

Keke Tariq excused himself and went into the shop to buy cigarettes and have a talk with the new guide. When he came back, we continued on foot, walking for more than half an hour on a different route, parallel to the one by which we had come. The farther we went, the more steeply the hills rose, until we came to a piece of rugged terrain immersed in its own silence. We followed a track that would alternately narrow and then widen. It did not appear well-trodden by anyone other than those on this sort of mission. It lay between two mountain ranges, which had in a different era perhaps been one mountain, split by an earthquake once upon a time, long ago. Keke Tariq asked me no questions as to the particulars of what concerned me. Most of the time, silence was our companion—his voice reaching me only with remarks about the path: "This way"; "Be careful of these jutting rocks"; "Don't be afraid if you hear wolves"; "Are you tired? You can rest here." I gave brief replies, my lips dry.

We descended into a deep valley, thick with evergreen cypress and stone pines, with their needled foliage and bifurcated trunks, while a pointillist design of blood-red anemones adorned the meadows and mountainsides. Keke Tariq made no comment, except to observe that we were now beyond the borders of Khanaqin. I didn't ask him where we were exactly, and after that I heard no more except the sound of the whirling winds, my own breath, the birds, and our footfalls upon the boulders. Startled by a wolf's howl, I would have lost my balance and fallen had I not clung to a tree trunk. Keke Tariq turned and, seeing how frightened I was, said, "It's a wolf—didn't I tell you there were a lot of them in this region? A wolf, Madame Narjis, and yet more merciful than human beings." He spoke of the wolf as if it were a rabbit, as he walked ahead of me with the surefooted gait of one well accustomed to tracks like this one, but slowly, so that I would be able to keep up with him. I remembered the words, "Yusef has not been devoured by wolves." What would make one wolf different from another? The howling stopped when the path curved to the left, still narrow and enclosed by mountains, by trees, by deep green. Now my ears picked up the murmur of water. Soon a clearing appeared amid the dense thicket of trees, where to the right of the track I could see it gushing from the mountaintops to the depths of the valley. Feeling thirsty, I asked to go and drink from the falling stream, and wash my face. I set my feet down carefully, for the rocks were covered in slippery mosses. How I wished I could penetrate to the heart of this waterfall and bathe beneath its heavenly cascade—perhaps it would cleanse me of my sorrows. As I washed my face, I heard Keke Tariq say, "You can rest a little while here. We've got a rough road ahead of us. Are you hungry?"

He took a sandwich from the bag of food, poured some tea into a paper cup, and moved a few meters away. Leaving the rest of the provisions for me and seating himself on a boulder, he nibbled at his sandwich and sipped his tea. I looked up at the clear sky and the mountaintops brilliantly illuminated by the sun. I watched the colorful birds, some of them flitting among the trees, others alighting on half-submerged rocks in order to quench their thirst. What if I had come here under other circumstances? How well I might have appreciated the magnificence of my surroundings!

I ate half of a cheese sandwich and drank some black tea. By this time Keke Tariq was smoking a cigarette. Gazing at the natural beauty of the place, and its inhabitants—God's creatures—harmonizing and blending in with one another, I said to him, "You live in a paradise here."

"A paradise, yes," was his reply, "but a paradise surrounded by a hell."

It occurred to me then to inquire about Umm Hani, so I asked him about the status of her mission. After a pull on his cigarette he said, "She is now under the care of one of our sheikhs. He will take over her case and try to find out what became of the matter after last year, when Kouran Delshad Bakhtiar was killed along with a number of others who were with him during one of the raids carried out by the authorities."

"What do you think, Keke Tariq—will she find her son?"

"There's no way of knowing that," he replied, "but what is most likely is that her son was also killed, in the same incident."

We fell silent for a few moments, while he finished smoking. He tossed his cigarette butt aside and stood up. "All right, let's get going."

Turning right, we began our ascent up the side of the bowl of the valley—we would have to climb a moderately high mountain. Keke Tariq increased our pace toward the mountain, while I cautiously made my precarious way along the path, unaccustomed as I was to climbing mountains or even hills. My feet had always trodden level ground; now here I was, clinging to sharp-pointed rocks whose savage teeth tried to snag everything, gasping for breath as my spirit shouldered its burden of hope: a long shot, to flush those miracles from their hiding places—where were they?

When we crested the mountain and started down the other side, the land seemed to open up, presenting a wide prospect of rolling terrain. Endowed by God with a fabulous beauty, the land offered up its subtle range of hues, its undulating slopes, its mountains in harmony with the greenery and the many-colored wildflowers that adorned them.

There was a car waiting for us, with a man standing near it. Keke Tariq raised his hand, wordlessly greeting him from a distance. The man moved toward us when he spotted us, and the two men reached to shake each other by the hand. Then Keke Tariq said to the other man, "I'm entrusting our sister Narjis to you."

With his thumb, the man pointed to his eyes, to indicate his assent, but he did not speak. Looking at him, I saw that he appeared to be in his mid-thirties, and that he was of moderate height. His tanned face was pock-marked, and on his right eyebrow was the trace of an old wound. Keke Tariq opened the car door, ushering me into the back seat, so I sat there and waited for him to get in beside the other man, but he turned to me and said, "Mr. Rushdie is your guide now. He is able to get to places that are hard to reach; he's the one who'll take you there and bring you back to where I'll be waiting for you."

There was something haughty about Rushdie's features. I did not ask where "there" was—everything that I had experienced so far was, to me, "there"—doubtless this Rushdie, like Mohsin al-Alwan, did his work for money; as was my habit with the guides, I didn't speak unless it was necessary. Before the car set off in the direction of those rugged roads, I gave him half of the sum agreed upon with Keke Tariq. Then he gave me a strip of black cloth and told me in clear Arabic to blindfold myself—so I did. I could no longer see anything, but I heard him say, "These are the rules of the game."

I thought to myself, "Have people's sorrows become a game in the hands of men like this, who trade in catastrophe?" And yes, a commercial transaction is what it is, and if they take money for it then they are merchants—a special class of merchants, whose commodities are well known, but outside the law, not on record. Money in exchange for learning the fate of those who've disappeared or been taken—whether they are alive or dead; a price based on what the trouble is—what sort of misfortune and how fraught with complications.

The car made uneven progress, traveling a rugged road, no doubt: the only alternative for the kind of task undertaken by the guides, who kept well away from heavily traveled routes. From time to time, though, with extreme caution, I pulled the blindfold aside and glanced furtively at the road, as if I meant to commit it to memory.

After perhaps half an hour, Rushdie said, "Take off the blindfold and get out of the car."

I removed the thing, and got out, with the sense that I was still surrounded by a passing twilight.

Rushdie parked the car between two trees that cast long shadows. After about a fifteen-minute walk, we climbed a rise, and in the distance a building appeared, its features difficult to make out. In five minutes we reached the fence behind the building, then went around, and it was before us: a one-story building, covered with dust-colored camouflage netting, which, from far away, resembled a range of low hills. It was guarded by a number of soldiers. I couldn't tell whether it was a prison or a police station, but in any case it was terrifying: its isolated location, the guards poised for action, the stone façade giving nothing away—and all that could not be divined about its character. What was behind that gate?

"Sit over here," said Rushdie, "until I come back."

The space was an abandoned corner. Scattered here and there were empty containers, nylon bags, cigarette butts, and perforated tin cans. I sat on a rock, where others before me had surely sat, enduring this painful wait. Time hung heavy, and my head was empty of everything. Perhaps I had emptied it of the past in order to be able to fill it with what was to come—which was what? The silence alone seemed an intrusion on the strange place; it was interrupted by the calls of large birds, which hovered low above the ground, then took off into the sky. Then there were the footfalls of the soldiers pacing the short distance between the gate and the passageway into which Rushdie had disappeared. I waited for whatever news of Yusef might come, even should it be that he was among the dead. Nothing could be more cruel than to spend the rest of your life wondering about the fate of a lost loved one: whether he was among the living, or whether death had in some manner taken him. In the case of the latter, a volcano of sorrow would erupt once, and engulf you; then, little by little it would subside, leaving nothing but memories, which would fade with the passage of time. Vacillation between certainty and doubt, on the other hand, was something that, in and of itself, seized hold of you and made a mockery of your life, planting in your viscera a tree of sorrows bearing bitter fruit for every season.

I started, not having heard Rushdie's footsteps before he spoke. "It'll be some time before we know anything." Seating himself on a rock, he lit a cigarette and sat smoking, not speaking to me until he'd finished it. Then he stood up and said, "I'll be back shortly."

He walked toward a tall, thin man who had emerged from the passageway, carrying some papers. They stood face-to-face, far enough away so that I was unable to hear any of their conversation. I watched closely as their lips formed speech, watched the movements of their hands and the papers through which the tall man was leafing in a leisurely fashion. Then they set off and disappeared into the passageway. I was beset by apprehensions, which picked me up and tossed me down into a well of anxiety and confusion, so oppressing me that I nearly stopped breathing, while a silent cry rose deep within me: "My God, when will the miracle come?"

Amid the worry and uncertainty, Yusef's face appeared before me: his face as it was in a different era, not this one. I saw him and myself sitting on a bench in the shade of a eucalyptus tree in Zawraa Park, when we had a run-in with a policeman. We weren't doing anything that violated "public decency and societal values," contrary to the allegation of the policeman, who stood scowling in front of us. He shook his finger in Yusef's face and shouted, "What are you two doing?"

I kept quiet, while Yusef addressed himself to the problem. "We're not doing anything," he said, "as you can see."

"The fact that the two of you are alone on this path can only mean that the third party present is the Devil."

"What devil do you mean, man?"

"I am a policeman and also a security officer. When you speak to me, you'd better remember that you're talking to a representative of the central authority!"

"Have you seen anything offensive to the nation's honor?"

"If I were not here in front of you, you would be committing some abominable act."

Riled up now, Yusef replied, "What's abominable is your suggestion. And you should know that we are engaged to be married, Mr. Central Authority."

"Are you making fun of me, boy? Give me your identity card."

Emerging from my silence, I said, "We apologize, sir—we have the utmost respect for your authority. Please pardon us this time—it won't happen again."

The policeman stepped back and directed his reply to Yusef. "I accept your apology," he said, "and now, get out of here, before I change my mind and arrest you, as I am fully authorized to do."

We left the park, but Yusef was angry with me. He said I was allowing them to humiliate us. I tried to defend myself, but he said, between clenched teeth, "He's nothing but a regular policeman. No doubt he's got no one to love him, so he takes his frustrations out on us. There was no need for you to apologize to him."

I tried to calm him down, reminding him of the man who'd been taken in by a policeman and whose girlfriend had run away, for fear of a scandal.

"Yes, I remember. They detained him for a month, but it wasn't because he was sitting among the trees with a woman—it was because he was under surveillance as a suspected Communist. The fact that he'd severed his connection to the party didn't make any difference."

Suddenly the scene changed, and I saw Yusef, agitated, nearly exploding with anger. "Why did you get married, Narjis? You couldn't wait?"

"Yusef, calm down—hear me out."

"No, I don't want to hear a word. Treachery runs in your veins, you women—your hearts are carved from stone. Your mother Eve was the first—she banished us from Paradise, and now here we are, in Hell for all eternity."

"In our mother Eve's time, there were no other men for her to betray our father Adam with. Nothing happened except that they ate the apple together—but never mind all that now. Look at me: I am Narjis, the woman you love, and I've come here, crossing mountains and valleys, leaving everything behind for your sake. My heart is not made of stone—it's soft as a flower petal. Remember our small delights—they were greater than all creation. Give me a chance, let me explain what happened."

But I did not get the chance, even there in the dream at whose edges I lingered, for it was interrupted by the cry of a raptor. Yusef's face vanished, returning me to the place in which I sat, monitoring the entrance to the passageway and the soldiers' footfalls and wondering what would happen if I really saw him—how would it be if I should see him? Would my having searched for him be enough to make him disregard my marriage?

Rushdie emerged from the passageway and hurried toward me, obviously bringing news. The moment he reached me he said, "His name is not on the lists, but there is a group of men with no names."

"With no names? Then how do they know them?"

"They have no need for names. Maybe they assign numbers to them, or the names of insects."

"Numbers? Insects?"

"Follow me, and don't ask questions. I got them to let you in. Whatever you can afford to pay, it will help with your case."

Rushdie was not diffident or hesitant in his conduct—he came across as someone who had done this kind of thing countless times before. At the entrance to the passageway, he introduced me to a fearsome-looking man: huge, dark, blunt-featured, and glowering, his expression sharp and savage like the visage of a hawk. Rushdie said he would wait for me.

Before the man took me into the gloomy anterooms, he had me sign a paper with a statement enjoining me to keep silent—to forget, once I left, anything I might see in this place; the alternative was a death sentence, as the document stipulated. It reminded me of the paper the officer who interrogated me in Baghdad had made me sign after Yusef disappeared. The tone in which he ordered me to read and sign the document was gruff, imperious, peremptory; I paid him what he demanded, and he shoved the money into his pocket, giving me a look as contemptuous as it was rude. Then he conducted me into the heart of the long, gray-tiled corridor.

The farther into the passageway we got, the dimmer grew the light. This corridor led to another, shorter one, then one of moderate length, and then we turned into a twisting passageway—it seemed as though there was no end to the corridors, and I felt as if we were being pulled down into the earth. Next we came to a set of iron staircases leading still farther down, the light by now all but extinguished. The big man preceded me, in his hand a flashlight, which he now switched on, there in the murk, the dampness, the heavy atmosphere of that place. A fetid stench hung in the air of those corridors; it was as if I was in the foulest of lavatories, and a voice like that of my mother shouted at me, "What is this hellish labyrinth you've wandered into, Narjis?"

I heard something like a continuous moaning, which ceased as we approached the iron door. The door opened when the big man pressed a button, and then we descended the four or five stone steps that led to a cellar in front of which was the first of two grates; the second of them stood about two meters beyond the first. The man advanced three or four steps and opened the first one, which yielded with a harsh squeal. He did not open the second one. "One minute only," he said, "and it is forbidden to speak with them." He switched off the flashlight.

There was a meager light, whose source I could not identify, which scarcely illuminated the place at all, but it sufficed for me to see the ghosts. These ghosts did not resemble those that used to appear before me in my childhood—these were the skeletons of men, or what appeared to be men, clinging to the earth. As soon as they heard the sound of the door being opened, or perhaps when they saw me, some of the bodies began to stir, to crawl across the tiles—or not tiles, rather, but just bare, colorless flooring. Their hair and beards were long, as if they lived in mediaeval times; and each of them seemed like a replica of a single man, a man bearing Yusef's features—or else Yusef had no features, or . . . this is how it seemed to me for the first moment; no doubt I was deceived by appearances. I opened my eyes wider and stared at them, that iron grate separating them from me: how many were they? Ten? Fifteen? More? Between emotional agitation and distorted vision, I could not be certain of their number. They clung together and seemed to multiply; their lips moved soundlessly, as if they had no tongues; their eyes were vacant, like hastily dug graves; they coughed, not as human beings do, but with a sound like labored, rasping breath emanating from a tomb. They gazed at me in sorrow, with the expression of one unable to believe that life aboveground still went on, or as if the woman who stood before them had descended upon them from another planet. Behind that grate their world had been annihilated—perhaps they had forgotten that they were human, for indeed they were now closer to animals in appearance, yet farther from animals, in their crushed and mortified souls. My God: How could a person—capable of laughter, of aspiration, of dreams—be so transformed, reduced to such ignominious frailty?

In a voice that rose from the depths of my anguish I said, "Yusef, my love, where are you?" Three men crawled toward me—they all looked identical; perhaps they were in fact one, splintered by the pain in my heart.

Now the big man admonished me. "I told you," he said, "do not talk to them. Point out the one you're looking for—that's it. Otherwise I'll put an end to this visit."

I pleaded with him, begging him to turn his flashlight back on and shine it on the men. He refused. He was about to yank me back, but in a flood of tears I clung to the bars. He turned on the flashlight and shone it on the faces of the men who had moved toward me. I found myself sinking to the floor, falling to my knees so that I could be directly in front of them. I struggled to keep ahold of the last filament of my consciousness, and not to lose my reason. I looked into their extinguished eyes, their distorted features, their bodies robbed of humanity: not by wars, but in fact by hands proficient in the making and prolonging of war. Bodies dead, notwithstanding the broken, feeble breaths still coming from somewhere deep within them. Before my eyes they multiplied; I felt dizzy and short of breath myself. Where was the air? I could barely breathe. Perhaps I was in Hell—I couldn't tell; I struggled to open my eyes and take a hard look at what was before me. With a sob, I asked: "Which of you is Yusef Hassan Omran?" None of them replied—they were like blind men, raising their heads to try to discern where the voice was coming from. The big man said, "Enough. If the one you're looking for were here, he would have answered you." At this moment I was straining my eyes to pick out every detail of their faces, and I concluded with certainty that Yusef was not among them. I would know Yusef, even if they had ruined his beautiful face.

I came out of the cellar, the big man behind me this time, as if he was afraid I might turn and go back to them—to those men without names, without lives. My soul was shattered, so much that a silent scream, heard only by me, rose within me: "Where is God, in all of this?"

I walked the corridors utterly spiritless, my eyes as bleary as if I had just emerged from the murk of a tomb. I stumbled as I went, as though walking on thorns that pierced my feet. I heard the big man say, "Goodbye," and I heard the cry of my heart, "'*Goodbye*'? Where is there any 'goodness' or peace?"

Hastily the man added, "And don't forget that you've signed a pledge."

Rushdie was waiting for me. I stumbled and nearly fell, even though I was trying to be careful. He asked me, "Was he there?"

"No," I replied. It hurt to speak. We walked back to the car. I don't know how I got in, how I resumed my place in the vehicle. Their faces pursued me; the echo of their moans pierced me. I shut my eyes to the verdant natural world God had created, so incongruous with the grotesqueries enacted in the interstices. I felt as though the core of me was collapsing, one thing toppling onto another. I heard stifled cries issuing from beneath the earth, or maybe from the sky above. Surely God must know what was happening in this dismal quarter of his kingdom—why then did he turn away? These men were, above all, his flock—how then could the shepherd leave his sheep to such a fate? So I asked myself, and then I asked God's forgiveness, struggling against my own weakness, so as not to crumble altogether; I begged for patience. Hope, though, had faded, its lamp extinguished in this crucial interval.

Once again I was blindfolded, and once more I was submerged in a vortex inhabited by those skeletal ghosts, the spectacle of which had been embedded in my brain like nails. I could see them crawling, hear their moans, which were echoed from within the depths of my being. With an enormous effort, I extricated myself from these visions. I had a sense of the road the car was traversing, which seemed rougher than the one by which we had come. I pulled aside the blindfold and stared at the road; noting that it was indeed a different one, I was seized by fear. What if this Rushdie should throw me from the vehicle and rape me, here in these parts so desolate of all human presence—and in the sight of God, no less—then order me to keep quiet about it, since I was a fugitive from the law? I put the blindfold back over my eyes, and, in a voice from which I was at great pains to remove any tremor of fear, I said "Excuse me, brother—the blindfold is hurting my eyes.

Without looking at me, he said, "Take it off, then. We're beyond the roads we're forbidden to use."

I pretended I was removing the blindfold for the first time. After a few moments, I said, "Is this the same road we came by?"

He told me the truth. "No," he said, "it's not the same one."

"Then where are we going now?"

"We haven't finished today's business," he said. "We're heading for a different location. Political prisoners are either in the building we just visited or in the hospital for the mentally ill."

A shiver ran through my body like an electrical current. I said, "I haven't come looking for a madman, Rushdie."

He replied coldly, "All the inmates are political dissidents, and you know very well what happens to them."

"No, I don't."

"They're driven insane."

"Why are they kept alive, then? Of what use is someone who's lost his mind?"

"They use them as subjects for experimentation. Lab rats, that is."

My God. How can a human being be turned into a rat? If what I saw in that building was human reptiles, would I, this time, have to see human rats? What sort of man was this Rushdie, and what were the other missions he undertook? And why was he divulging such dangerous secrets? I said to myself, "Endurance—I call on endurance to help me through this . . . patience come to my aid, so long as I must absorb the things I've seen, the things I've heard." I said to Rushdie, "I don't know whether or not I'll be able to stand what I'm going to see."

"Women's hearts are weak," he said, with a hint of scorn. "In any case, I'm the one who'll be going inside—not because you wouldn't be strong enough to take it, but because the directives are strict here, and they don't allow strangers inside."

"So you're close to them—meaning one of them?" These words I said only in my mind, not letting them past the barrier of my tongue. Instead I let out a breath, a sigh like the first of a lifetime, and prepared myself for a new ordeal. I hoped that Yusef would not be among the "rats."

I was still caught up in the realm of human ghosts when we arrived at the hospital. The ghosts kept

moving toward me, moaning, the whole time Rushdie was gone—perhaps fifteen minutes or more. I no
longer understood time in minutes or hours, having
given up wearing my watch, which had stopped without warning. Time expanded, proportionate to the
magnitude of the sorrows enclosed within my heart.

My gaze followed him as he walked to the hospital entrance, his shadow following him; momentar-
ily disoriented, I could no longer distinguish Rushdie
from his shadow. I had reached a point of such exhaustion, I could no longer endure it—yet, remembering the sufferings of Umm Hani I withstood it
patiently.

This building could not be a hospital, even if its
façade presented it as such—no doubt that was for
camouflage, since its inmates were dissidents. The
building was like the one we'd visited before it: situ-
ated in an area isolated from houses and government
offices, surrounded by concrete walls and barbed
wire, secured by an iron door no different from that
of a prison. What was behind it, God alone knew;
no one was coming out or going in, only my guide
standing at the door. He stood there for some minutes
before a man came and opened it for him without
hesitation. It was clear that they had already seen him
with some sort of special equipment, and that he was
known to them. I was once more assailed by the faces
of those wrecks of men, beset by those bodies about
to give out: their nakedness, their mortification,
the desecration of their manhood, the annihilation

of their humanity. I felt a burning sensation in my stomach, a bitterness on my tongue, while my eyes remained fixed upon the door. What might lie behind such insanity?

As Rushdie went into the building and disappeared, I entered a new nightmare, in which I saw Yusef blindfolded, bound hand and foot, his mouth taped shut. Heartless men wheeled him into a room on a gurney, from which they hoisted him onto a bed in the center of the room, with spotlights trained on it. Then they busied themselves with a bunch of tubes, which they arranged on various parts of his body. One of them held a large syringe, like those used on animals, containing some yellow liquid. He plunged the needle into a muscle in Yusef's arm, putting him into a deep sleep in a matter of seconds. At this point, the chief of these men noticed me in the doorway and moved angrily toward me. He slammed the door shut, and I could no longer see anything. While I waited, time passing but making no sense, the scene suddenly changed, bringing me back to the present. The gate opened, and Rushdie came hurrying out. He got into the car, tossing in my direction a single sentence, then fell into a protracted silence.

"The only person by the name of Yusef at this hospital," he said, "is Yusef Qasim Damin, not Yusef Hassan Omran."

Was I to thank God that my beloved Yusef was neither one of the skeleton-ghosts nor among the lab rats?

The car set off, heading back by the same route as before. The trees no longer looked green, but had turned a somber gray. The guide did not speak to me, except briefly and intermittently, but the question escaped my lips: "How do they use human beings as lab rats?"

As coldly as before, Rushdie replied, "They run trials on them in order to learn the effects of biological experiments and germ warfare, the symptoms of exposure to chemical weapons, such as stomach ailments. Haven't you heard about this?"

My lips moved—I wanted to come up with something other than that I didn't know what to say, but I held my tongue and he, for his part, kept silent. What sort of man was he, I wondered? I was at a loss to classify him. Was he one of them, or was he against them? If he was one of them, how could he give away their secrets? And if he was against them, why did he deal with them? Or could it be that he was playing both ends against the middle, as they say, that nothing mattered to him but the money, and that others cooperated with him, likewise for the sake of money?

It was early afternoon by the time the car stopped. I saw Keke Tariq sitting in the shade of a pine tree, smoking a cigarette. It was as if he'd been frozen in place from the time we left. As soon as he caught sight of the car, he stood up to greet me. The guide got out of the car and opened the door for me. I picked myself up and got out.

"Good news, my sister Narjis?" said Keke Tariq.

Rushdie replied in my stead. "We didn't find him, either at the detention center or at the mental hospital."

I looked from one to the other of them, then asked, "Is that the end of the mission?"

Keke Tariq gave Rushdie a look that demanded a response. Rushdie turned to me. "Maybe you've come too late," he said. "The accused are usually moved from one place to another without their names being entered into the lists. What made you wait so long, and then come now to look for him?"

"I thought he was dead," I said, my voice breaking. "It was a tip that he was still alive that brought me here, belatedly."

"There's one last chance," he said, "at learning the fate of a detainee, but it needs time."

I looked into his eyes, searching them for what lay behind the words he'd spoken. I said nothing, in case he wanted to finish his statement by asking for money.

The silence lasted only a moment, and then he said, "One of those I work with told me that from time to time they take bodies and bury them in secret, in some unknown location."

"And how can we know the names of those who were buried," Keke Tariq asked, "and where they are?"

"We can find out their names," said Rushdie. "The difficulty lies in finding out where they were buried."

Keke Tariq spoke again. "When will we know the names?"

"When I receive them from the source," Rushdie replied.

"And if he's not among those who were interred?"

"Then they'll have moved him to some other place, in absolute secrecy."

12

We had to go back the way we had come, so we climbed the mountain once more, Keke Tariq and I. He was trying to instill in me a beguiling hope. "We haven't exhausted all our resources yet. We have groups that work in Sulaymaniyah, in Duhok, in Irbil, in Kirkuk."

I didn't ask him to explain what he meant by his reference to "resources" that had not yet been exhausted, here or elsewhere. My own reserves of strength were too depleted for me even to carry on a conversation. I didn't think I would recover. I felt as though something was spreading through my joints—pain, perhaps, emanating from my heart and distributing itself throughout my body—when I thought about the turn my mission had taken. For I had come seeking a living man of flesh and blood, and all it had come to was that I should know where his body lay; there was just a faint hope that he might have been detained in some other place. I felt, in this moment, as though I was not myself, that the hands of time were moving backward, even though I had turned my back on the past and left it behind.

Exhaustion overtook me utterly, and I clung to the stone. The mountain seemed to stretch endlessly before me, as if it was not the same mountain I had climbed a few hours earlier, as if its outcroppings had been transformed into knife-blades that cut my fingers and drew blood. Cautiously I held onto the solid stone, holding my breath lest my fingers should slip; then, the moment I got hold of the topmost section of rock, I drew breath ever so slowly, fearful that my fingers might move and lose their grip. What if I were to tumble down, strike my head on a rock, and die here?

As we descended toward the valley on the other side of the mountain, I felt a sense of vertigo. I slowed down, so as not to fall into the abyss—wasn't the abyss in which I already dwelt enough? The base of the mountain was a long way off, and it seemed to me that the rocks under my feet were unstable. I drew breath cautiously, trying not to hyperventilate, and before I had got much closer to the bottom, I was dizzy. Everything around me danced, shifting and toppling down on me: the mountains, the sloping ground, the trees, the rocks, the streams—everything. My consciousness was slipping, down, down, and I struggled against the fainting fit that was trying to insinuate itself into my limbs. Closing my eyes, I called out to Keke Tariq, who hurried over and helped me down the rest of the way, to where the waterfall was.

"Wash your face," he told me, "and rest." Then he turned aside to smoke a cigarette.

How I wished in that moment that I could throw myself into the water, that eternal substance, becoming one of the droplets of which it consisted and disappearing forever. Thus I would enter into timelessness, effaced within the torrent, never to rejoin humankind.

When I regained my equilibrium, I was unable to stem the tide of tears that burst forth. Keke Tariq approached and sat down on a rock surrounded by ferns. He passed his fingers over the broad fronds, as if searching among them for words. When he found them, he said, in an effort to soothe me, "Calm yourself—tears won't accomplish anything or change the way things are."

Overcome by despair, I said, "What does change them, then? And what am I to do in the coming days? I can't go back to Baghdad—if you know the details of my story, then you know that I left it while I was under orders to stay put. What am I to do, Keke Tariq?"

"You are safe," he said. "You are under our protection, and you won't go back until you find a solution that satisfies you. Besides, there is a question that still hasn't been resolved, namely that of the detainees who reached the security forces' headquarters in Sulaymaniyah. It's nearly impossible, of course, but we'll try everything we can to find out their names."

"Why didn't you tell this to Rushdie? Didn't you say that he has ways of getting at what is all but inaccessible?"

"Rushdie is a specialist operating within specific constraints, and Sulaymaniyah doesn't fall within his remit."

He was quiet for a while. I watched his expression, in case it might tell me something to quell the unease that had taken root in me. Then he turned his gaze on the unknown horizon, to speak of other things.

"You know, Madame Narjis, I'm the only member of my family who escaped when the regime deployed chemical weapons against Halabja. At the time, I was working in Panjun, in Sulaymaniyah, and when I got home I found no one. Thousands of bodies had been buried, and thousands more had been devoured by dogs and carrion birds. Some of these were still alive, moaning in their final moments, as the dogs tore into their flesh—then, even the dogs became corpses. After a wearying search, I found the bodies of my father, two of my brothers, and my older sister. I never found my mother or my brother, who was still nursing. A year later, though, by chance, I received—secretly—a magazine from a friend who had fled the country. Among the many photographs I found a picture of my dead mother, my brother in her arms. Beneath the picture my friend had written to say that her image had become like a poster, circulating among the foreign news agencies. I still keep the magazine in a hidden spot, buried in the ground, for fear it might fall into the hands of the authorities. They wanted to wipe us off the face of the earth."

The river of tears had stopped, and I felt ashamed. It alarmed me, too, that, because of a media cover-up, we had not known the magnitude of the Anfal tragedy. Everything had been, and still was, concealed from us, what with travel prohibited, satellites banned—as for cell phones, we had heard of them, but we didn't even know what they looked like. And the world was a devil. It was mute.

We started walking again, slowly. When we got to Houshyar's shop once more, Keke Tariq called his nephew Sirwan, while I sat in the shade of a mulberry tree. He brought me a bowl of kefir and some bread, but I handed the bread back to him as I was thirsty, not hungry. While Keke Tariq sat in a chair in front of the shop, talking with its owner, I was seized by a cyclone of images. They took me back to that strange building, to the skeletons creeping along the bare floor, to a world of tormented spirits and unendurable agonies. These were crowded out by new images, of things I hadn't seen with my own eyes, but with my imagination: images of the bodies devoured by dogs and carrion birds, then the dogs that themselves became corpses. I could even, almost, hear the groans unheard by the heavens, to which I flung my question: "Dear God, why would you let anyone who worships you suffer such cruelty?"

I was so exhausted I was gasping for breath; I lost all sense of the passing minutes, my body was not my own, and time stood still in every recess of my being, until I could no longer feel anything. It was as if I was not human, merely something amorphous that existed outside of time. This was how I felt at the moment when I awoke and found myself in the guest quarters, after a night of heavy sleep penetrated by brief and troubled moments of waking that disrupted my rest. I emerged from a strange dream, in which I had seen Yusef. I was walking along a road, trying to outpace my elongated shadow, which stretched before me, when his voice startled me, issuing from somewhere in front of me. Seeing me had caught him by surprise.

"What are you doing here, Narjis?"

His surprise was contagious. "I came looking for you!"

It didn't strike me as odd when he said, "But I'm not in this city."

"Where are you, then?" I asked him.

"I'm in the City of No-place," he replied.

I could have asked him where this city was, but some sound propelled me out of that dream, or perhaps what I had had was a waking dream, and it had roused me. I struggled to open my eyes, and saw Mizgin carrying a thermos bottle and two glasses. She told me that she had checked on me more than once while I was deeply asleep.

Still disoriented from my dream, I pressed my fingers to my temples and tried to massage away the pain that had set in. I asked Mizgin for some tablets that might alleviate the headache.

"Pills won't do anything," she said. "I've made you an herbal drink." She handed it to me, and I drank it down; it had a bitterness to it, but not the soul-crushing kind. She poured some for herself as well. "You'll feel better after this," she said. "It's a pain-relieving infusion for headache, and it boosts blood circulation."

I waited for her to ask me about my journey, but she didn't. It seemed Keke Tariq must have told her about it, and she needed no further explanation from me. "Everything will be all right," she said, pouring more of the herbal drink for me. Not knowing what to say, I kept quiet. The tears receded from my eyes, retreating behind the edges of pain in my head; so disappointment was prevented from taking over the reins of my fate, but my tired eyes betrayed the sense of defeat—was it possible for disappointment to show so clearly as to be obvious even to an uncomplicated woman like Mizgin? Evidently so, for she came closer to me and patted my shoulder, in an effort to ease my distress. She smiled, and said confidently, "Truth grows ill, but it will not die."

I found myself joking with her, although without returning her smile. "You should give it some of your herbal infusion, then, so that it can recover more quickly." But privately I wondered, "What good is the truth if it's sick? And what good is a body whose owner is no longer alive?"

The herbal infusion helped me concentrate, and got my blood moving, but it didn't dispel my sense of loss. I said to Mizgin, "I see that my problem now is my own dilemma. I can't go back to Baghdad, so maybe I'll flee the country, and leave it to the Refugee Agency to find some other homeland for me."

The idea of starting over in a new country had not just that moment occurred to me. I had thought of it when I was held captive between one terror and another. The notion had struck me after I emerged from that frightful tunnel behind the wall of the guest quarters, but hadn't taken shape so clearly in my mind.

Mizgin objected. "One doesn't just trade in one's homeland," she said. "In the land of one's fathers and grandfathers, the hawthorn is sweeter than figs."

Despite the sorrow in which I was sunk, I nearly laughed, not at the proverb, but at her persistence in using proverbs to back up what she said. "But Madame Mizgin," I said, "I feel lost. The land of my ancestors no longer cares for me, whether with hawthorn or with figs."

"Don't say that. As long as you are with us, you're not lost. Your mission isn't completed yet—so I understood from Keke Tariq and my husband Mahmoud when they were talking things over. Keke Tariq doesn't leave people in the lurch, but I don't know what he's planning next."

As she was leaving the room, I said, "I'm longing for sleep."

"Rest," she said. "I won't wake you until dinner time."

I wasn't badly in need of sleep, but I wanted it, in the hope of finishing my interrupted conversation with Yusef, so I could ask him, "Where is this City of No-place?"

13

A few days later, Keke Tariq told Narjis, in Mizgin's presence, that she was to move to Sulaymaniyah, for here it was no longer safe. News had spread that a wide-ranging security sweep would be carried out in Khanaqin, following the arrest of an officer, so it was best that she be in a place of safety. Keke Tariq himself would conduct her to one of the mountain villages not far from Iran. Mizgin told her that these villages were safer because they were so far outside the cities. Thus began, for Narjis, yet another journey whose outcome she could not know.

Keke Tariq did not delay; he arrived early the following morning, before sunrise. He and Narjis set off for Sulaymaniyah, conveyed there by his nephew Sirwan along a tortuous route well away from the better-traveled main roads. It took three hours—perhaps more, for her sense of the minutes contained in an hour no longer functioned. They traveled through lofty mountains, streams that cascaded from the mountaintops, and endless, magnificent green forest. But how could she delight in their splendor or appreciate the divine beauty of the place, with troubled spirits nesting in her head like birds of ill omen? It was a journey beset with perils—her mind would not let go of its foreboding; the foreboding itself was fraught with danger.

Occasionally a question would surface in her mind, and she would whisper to herself, "What have I done? I'm a woman who has nothing to do with politics. All I want is find out the truth about the disappearance of a man I love. So why does this terror seize me every time I move from one place to another?" Then she would think how differently matters really stood: The fear was justified, for if she should fall into the hands of the authorities, she would face she knew not what accusations, as they would probe beneath her skin for what they sought, not for what was there in the first place. What was under her skin would seem laughable to them. What was this "love" she spoke of? And how could she sell her country for the sake of a man who worked in opposition to it, for some ludicrous notion called "love"? Who had brought her here, first of all? How could she take the risk of entering forbidden territory, if she was not a party to activities on the order of "high treason and threats to national security"?

Were her own misgivings actually whispering to her? Had her apprehensions overtaken her to such an extent? Or were they magnified because her reserves of patience were so depleted?

Fear is a knotty place, like an ancient tree, thousands of years old, grown tall, with branches intertwined and spreading infinitely: an otherworldly realm, yet familiar to those upon whom it creeps up like a viper seeking food from the heart and mind of its prey. It strikes, injecting its paralyzing venom into its victim's body. Narjis tried, though, as best she could, with what remained of her patience, her strength of will, her dreams, to fend off the menace of that viper: no going back, no surrender—she was here because she had seen no other way of shaping her own destiny.

And now she had arrived at a certain village, called Qaladze, to the north of the city of Sulaymani-yah, not far from the Iranian border. It was enclosed by mountains, which she found somewhat reassuring. Meanwhile, she might, at the right time, cross the border in the event she should find herself at an impasse as to her mission here, for in Iran, Keke Tariq had informed her, there were expedients not yet exhausted. She didn't know how much time she would spend here before she could feel at ease about the safety the place offered to her. It had not previously crossed her mind to flee to Iran; she had held to an idea that, should circumstances compel her to leave the country, she would sneak into Turkey. Keke Tariq, however, had advised her that—given the region's proximity to the border—the shortest and safest routes were those that led to Iran. He further explained that there, in Iran, were people who would concern themselves with her situation, and guide her to the offices of the Refugee Agency. He held at the same time an alternate view of the question of her once again taking flight, for conditions in the country warned that a new war was brewing, which might be a game changer. Narjis herself, at bottom, was not enthusiastic about the idea of fleeing yet again. Her life had not been guaranteed against ill consequence in Khanaqin; hence it was insecure in Qaladze as well, albeit slightly less so, for she felt that the solidity of the surrounding mountains would protect her—but for how long?

Narjis took up residence in a stone house consisting of three rooms, at the foot of a mountain swathed entirely in green. Her hostess, whose name was Roujda, was a member of Keke Tariq's family, child of a Kurdish father and an Arab mother. Possessed of a cheerful disposition, she seemed to be bursting with life. She was a widow, her husband having lost his footing while climbing and fallen into the valley far below the mountain. She lived with her thirteen-year-old son, Shirwan, and worked a small vegetable farm, right behind her house, that she had inherited from her husband. Her brother Dileir came by each week and loaded produce from the farm onto two mules, for the place was not easily accessible by car. Then he proceeded to the nearby villages and sold the produce directly, sidestepping government regulations on trade. In this he was assisted by Shirwan, who also worked with him on a poultry farm. Narjis, so as not to sit idle before this hard-working woman, began to contribute her own labor to the enterprise. She harvested grapes by the bunch, as well as cucumbers, melons, and apples, gathering them into baskets and small sacks, just as Roujda did. She scattered seed or leftover scraps of food in front of the chicken coop and collected eggs from the nests. Five laying hens and a rooster occupied a chicken-wire enclosure in the shade of an enormous holm oak.

Narjis was struck by the abundance of copper and brass objects displayed in Roujda's house. When Roujda noticed her examining them, she said, "I like such things. I usually get them at the Safafir Market whenever we visit Baghdad, and I'm careful to make sure that they're connected with the history of Iraq. It's a hobby I picked up from my mother. You'll find something in every nook and cranny: the Ziggurat, the Lion of Babylon, the Spiral Minaret of Samarra, the Hanging Gardens, Lamassu the Sumerian Bull, and household utensils like the samovar, coffee and tea pots, plates, lamps, incense burners, vials for rosewater, and so forth. You'll like them."

The night of Narjis's arrival in Qaladze, she didn't sleep until the final hours before the dawn of another day, as was her habit on coming to an unknown place and covering herself with unfamiliar blankets. She woke at cockcrow, chill September breezes entering through the open window and stirring the thin curtains. She turned over in bed, conscious of her fatigue. Then she got up, washed her face in cold water, and went to the window, which overlooked the chicken coop. The rooster stopped crowing and approached the hens—he was a big, white fellow, crowned with a red crest and displaying long, golden tailfeathers. He strutted about in the midst of the hens, selected one of them—the only white one—and mounted her, grasping her neck with his beak and spreading his wings over her, coupling with her before his audience of four envious brown hens. They would never stop following him around, fawning over his wings and his proud tail, as if he were a sultan of his time, and they his slave-girls. From the depths of her sadness, a smile emerged and found its way to Narjis's lips—and as quickly faded.

Narjis was living in a state of anxious ambivalence, whether to leave the country or stay where she was, supposing there was an interval of safety for her among the Kurds. And once she understood the benign intentions of those who had taken her in, in her heart of hearts she was not inclined to leave. Rather she kept hoping for news—not suggested by the events of recent days—that Yusef might have been detained in the headquarters at Sulaymaniyah. This was no more than a pretext for staying: only a fond wish, for she knew that hope was slim, but she preferred to cling to an illusion rather than venture into the unknown in some other country. In Roujda she had found a most compatible person, for Roujda spoke with an

Arabic accent, and never stopped singing while at her work on the farm. She had memorized a great many Arab and Iraqi songs, and would urge Narjis to join in singing parts of them with her. She would laugh so heartily, it seemed that nature had endowed her with the secret to a simple delight that enabled her to live her life in gladness and contentment. She said to Narjis, "As the saying goes, 'A house full of joy cannot be destroyed.'" Then she would resume her singing. It seemed to Narjis, as time went by, that her own state of mind was improving. After much thought, she concluded that flight outside the country would be another sort of death, one that would creep up on her slowly. So she applied herself intently to her work with Roujda, and as the days passed, she stopped feeling beholden for the hospitality she'd been given, compensating it by her labor on the farm. She did not speak openly of her wish to stay, but left matters to take care of themselves. Whenever she imagined fleeing the country, she remembered Mizgin's hawthorn proverb and its meaning. And along came Roujda to reinforce her conviction that it was best to stay put.

"It's hard to change one's skin," she said. "Flight from one's own country is like a cancer, eating silently away at the body before devouring it once and for all."

But at times when Narjis found herself losing hope, she wished that dreadful illness would in fact devour her once and for all.

One day followed another, until something happened that no one had foreseen: news that was received with various degrees of credulity, doubt, and astonishment. All of a sudden the regime had invaded and annexed Kuwait. In the dead of night, a military convoy had crossed the border like a thief taking cover in darkness to prey upon its victim. The people of Kuwait had awakened to a hideous nightmare from which they found no escape, since they could make no more sense of it than could the civilians of Iraq. Government buildings were plundered of all they contained, as were people's homes, banks, national institutions—everything within reach of the regime, which disregarded all official demands that it leave Kuwait. The nightmare went on for seven months, while the two countries waited for the womb of the oppressor to deliver the liberation it promised. And at last it was delivered: the start of a new life for Kuwait, but for Iraq the amplified misery of an already wretched life.

The world had chosen to restore to one country its rightful sovereignty; and yet this same world, having called for an uprising against Iraq's leader, turned a blind eye to the rights of its defenseless people, who confronted a savage fate. While the leader stayed put, the populace suffered the effects of the longest trade embargo in the nation's history.

There were those killed in Kuwait, and others who were imprisoned; whoever was able to get out of the country got out; meanwhile, soldiers—embittered, exhausted, worn out, hungry, angry, and fed up with him who had driven them to their destruction—sold their rifles to the arms dealers who had suddenly materialized, trading them in for the sake of a glass of tea, a crust of bread, or a cigarette. And then a volcano of rage erupted.

The spark that ignited the uprising appeared in Saad Square, in Basra. It began with a soldier, who had recently sold his rifle, only to reclaim it and make for the presidential palace, there to discharge his ammunition and his anger into one of its walls. The gunshot found its echo in chanting and singing and calls for the downfall of the regime. The returning soldiers and the unarmed civilians, boiling over with fury, proceeded to the government buildings, the armories, and the headquarters of the party apparatus. They seized control of everything, and Basra fell into their hands. The spark ignited in other cities, blazing up in the governorates of Maysan, Dhi Qar, al-Diwaniyah, Muthanna, Babel, Wasit, Najaf, and Karbala. It proceeded northward, and spread from Ranya—not far from Sulaymaniyah—whose roads opened up, and burst the floodgates of bottled-up anger. The agitated throng made its way to the security headquarters, the prisons, and the center of party operations; the rebels freed prisoners, killed the director of Amna Suraka— the red building in Sulaymaniyah known as the "Red Jail," run by Iraqi security services—and rounded up the party adherents and killed them as well, whether with gunfire or whatever was at their disposal, which paved the way for the uprising to cross into Duhok, Kirkuk, and Irbil. These cities were no longer under the control of the regime.

The time Narjis had to spend waiting for Keke Tariq, or anyone who might fetch him for her, was excruciating. She wanted to get to the security head-quarters in Sulaymaniyah—the Red Jail. Waiting had become intolerable. She spoke to Dileir. "Take me with you by mule," she pleaded, "—take me to any place from which I can get to the headquarters."

He objected strenuously. "You have no idea what's going on," he said. "It's absolute chaos, nonstop gun-fire on every road. How would you get to the Green Zone? You'd better wait for Keke Tariq."

Narjis reluctantly gave way, but she asked Dileir to contact Keke Tariq by any means possible.

After several days, it seemed to Narjis that she was out of the holding pattern: Keke Tariq arrived. He was exhausted, however, and not enthusiastic about taking her to the Red Jail. In an effort to persuade him, she told him she was no longer afraid—that she was in full possession of the strength and courage she might need to face what was in store for her. He was emphatically opposed. He explained to her that things were in turmoil, and that no one knew what they might come to. Military personnel were fleeing, were abandoning their barracks, and were prepared to open fire on anyone they found suspicious; bod-ies, whether of the guilty or the innocent, were piling up in the streets; snipers on the rooftops were firing indiscriminately on those who passed below them; party loyalists, fleeing their posts, were chased down and killed by citizens taking their revenge—their corpses, too, still littered the streets.

"The killing has put the killers on notice," Roujda put in. "The dead—they deserved what happened to them."

"I don't believe in blind justice," Keke Tariq objected. "Murder begets murder."

"Aren't that lot implicated in the murder of your family?" said Roujda, clearly mystified.

Keke Tariq lit a cigarette, then said, "If we all take vengeance into our own hands, the chaos will never end."

"So you relinquish your rights?" said Roujda, in disbelief.

He drew deeply on his cigarette and blew the smoke toward the ceiling. "I won't give up my rights, of course," he said, "but I'll win them by legal means."

Roujda grew agitated. "How can you expect someone who has watched his wife or his sister raped before his eyes—raped and subjected to all manner of torture—to forget?" she demanded. "Do you expect him to deny his own feelings, and just say, 'The past is over and done with, and God will provide'?"

Keke Tariq took two puffs of his cigarette before he replied. "I'm not suggesting that the past is over and done with," he said. "And I don't ask victims to deny their feelings or erase their own memories. What I hope is that they may restrain their feelings so that the laws can take their proper course."

Glaring at Keke Tariq, Roujda spoke sharply. "What laws are you talking about, Keke Tariq?" she said. "Did they kill us in accordance with the laws? Haven't our forefathers said to us, since time immemorial, 'An eye for an eye, a tooth for a tooth, and he who has inflicted the injury must suffer likewise'?"

Narjis wanted, as the discussion heated up, to change the subject before it came to a quarrel. "Do you think this uprising will put an end to the regime?" she asked Keke Tariq.

"That depends," he said, crushing out the butt of his cigarette in an ashtray, "on the strength and staying power of the rebels."

Roujda was eager to renew the debate. "It seems," she said, "that you, too, have lost your hope and your will."

Refusing to rise to the bait, Keke Tariq replied calmly. "If I had lost my hope and my will," he said, "I would be among the dead."

Then he closed the door on the discussion, standing up and saying, "I've got to get back. I have a lot of obligations to attend to."

14

Here there were no means by which to witness what was happening around the world. The benefits of the satellite, the Internet, the mobile phone—these were still scarce here. The broadcast news reported Iraq's losses in Kuwait, but the trail of death that led from Basra to the other cities was obscure. The foreign media would say that the regime had collapsed, and that the rebels would now seize the reins of control, since the cities of Iraq had fallen, one after another, into their hands. That would then be directly contradicted by the only television station there was—until the rockets silenced it. This left only one alternative: the mobile media, which propagated zealous songs, songs of the great victory, the defeat of the enemy, the rout of the riffraff driven by forces that wished nothing good for the country. Whom to believe?

Since a lie is a short and flimsy cord, it was inevitable that the truth should come out, sooner or later. The news that reached this isolated village, though, was scant and incomplete. Roujda picked up bits and pieces from passersby, but what she learned was evidently conjectural, for each report was prefaced by the words, "They say . . ." The rumors accumulated, until Dileir no longer knew anything, for he had stopped going to the city center, on account of the upheaval and in fear of random gunfire. In such an atmosphere, whiffs of bad news were blown about unchecked.

A week after his first visit, Keke Tariq returned to Qaladze, taking Narjis by surprise. She was out on the farm, pruning young trees, when Roujda called to her from the kitchen window and let her know that he had come. Narjis dropped everything and ran. She found him sitting on a chair under the grape arbor by the door to the house. She greeted him anxiously, looking intently into his eyes and studying the contours of his face, the lines in his brow, more deeply furrowed now than before. She sensed that these features bore something of ill consequence to her— sensed it with all the misgivings he conveyed, for he averted his eyes each time they met hers. Yet his eyes gave it away, some piece of news he did not know how to deliver. After an interval of silence loaded with the significance of what was to come, Narjis asked him, in a faint voice, "Keke Tariq, what are you keeping from me?"

He turned his gaze skyward, as if asking for help from above with what he was about to tell her. He lit a cigarette and inhaled, then assembled his words.

"The country is on fire," he said. "I'm now on an ad hoc committee whose mission is to gather up documents so that they don't get lost. The citizens are riled up, and there are no more security centers or party offices that they have not penetrated. Some of them stole anything they happened to see in the dossiers, with the intention of hiding them, or else burning them so as to obliterate evidence that would support accusations of collaboration with the security apparatus. Others stole documents in order to sell them later on, exploiting the families of victims for profit. So we assembled this committee in order to preserve whatever documents are left."

He stopped speaking. Narjis fixed her gaze on his lips, on his features, the grimace that concealed something awful. The silence stabbed her to the heart with a savage blade. Keke Tariq took several puffs of his cigarette before continuing.

"We made copies of some of the documents that listed, specifically, the names of those condemned to death, and we posted them on the fronts of the buildings where they were found."

Narjis braced herself as he reached into his jacket pocket and drew out a piece of paper. "Madame Narjis," he said, "here is the document that pertains to you."

It was difficult for her to grasp the slip of paper, for she was trembling in every nerve and fiber. It slipped from her fingers as soon as they touched it, and fell to the ground. Keke Tariq bent to retrieve it and handed it to her once more. "I know how difficult this is for you," he said. "Please accept my condolences."

She kept silent, as if all creation were with her in silence; she felt ravaged and broken, felt as if her heart were knocking against her sides, trying to escape her ribs. In silence a wellspring of tears opened up and flowed in torrents—originating where, she did not know: from her eyes, from her wounded heart, or her battered soul. As she stared at the paper, the chair would no longer support her weight, and she fell to her knees. She searched for something that might explain Yusef's execution, and found nothing. It was as if she had never prepared herself for such an outcome, even though she had acknowledged that he was, in all probability, dead. As her tears continued to fall, she held the paper close to her face: just seven names, preceded by a verdict announcing the death penalty for each of them, but no mention of any reason. How had they been executed? By hanging? The firing squad? Had they been thrown from mountaintops—a method of which she had heard in this place? Had they been starved to death? Or had they been buried alive, in the desert, in the wilderness, under government buildings?

Roujda brought tea and placed it gently upon a small table. In the face of the silence that engulfed Narjis and Keke Tariq, she was mute as well. It seemed that time stood still, poised upon Narjis's lips and her hands as they clutched the slip of paper, her eyes fixed on number seven: Yusef Hassan Omran—his name, just that: as if he had sprouted and grown before her, like a tree, but only brushed her like a passing breeze that leaves behind nothing but its scent and an ardent wish to hold onto it. He was no more, as if he had never entered the world; or else he had entered it, but in the form of a dream that ends in a nightmare.

She spoke at last, halting words in a broken voice. She asked Keke Tariq to find a way of conveying the document to Mukhlis Farouq, for only he might know how to track down Yusef's family. He promised her that, as soon as a way could be found, he would send a copy.

To grasp that Yusef was no longer among the living would take time exceeding her forbearance. At every turn she had held at bay the likelihood that he was gone, in case miracles still happened on earth. Now that she held in her hand the evidence of his death, she must keep him alive in her heart: she must breathe him in with the air; see him in the green of the meadows, which reminded her of his eyes, and in the dense forests that lay upon the land. She whispered to him, in his eternal absence, that she had never loved, and would never love, any man but him.

Here we stand, upon the threshold of a new tragedy—or rather, we enter into the core of the tragedy. For despite the fact that three-quarters of the country had wrested itself free of the regime's tyranny, the insurrection was thwarted. The allied nations that had at first given their blessing to the uprising in short order reversed course, shifting the balance. Politics is a matter of vested interests, and in this moment—in the finer calculus of the moment—the nations' vested interests lay on the side of preserving the regime. Thus they did not stop at merely looking on as the regime massacred its people; they actually allowed it to use airpower to put down the revolt. The regime, for its part, did not stop short of using weapons prohibited by international law. Its forces advanced upon the cities, with the object of wrestling them back into submission with all the cruelty for which the regime was well known; thus tyranny came back to life like the proverbial nine-lived cat.

From that point forward, the country underwent the worst of the blockade, of torture and repression. The cities of Kurdistan, however, were granted some relief by the international community, inasmuch as American forces were stationed in Zakho to protect it. Kurdistan did not entirely escape control of the regime, but security forces and party apparatchiks no longer had a presence there.

15

Narjis breathed: air free of anxieties. She was no longer a prisoner of the house and farm, but took to going
out fearlessly, sometimes accompanying Dileir on his
rounds to sell produce in the city center. Her plan to
flee to Iran became a thing of the past, but she could
not so much as think of returning to Baghdad, after
what had happened. Who was there for her in that
place? There would be nothing but memories, which,
with all their attendant agonies, she could honor better by preserving them in her mind. Occasionally she
thought about Mukhlis Farouq, and what might have
become of him: Was he still at his bookshop, inhaling
the aroma of books, there on Mutanabbi Street? Did
his life flow like a tranquil river bordered by thorny
hedges of fear? Did he remember her, and wonder
where she was now, what she was doing?

What she had to do now was get through each
day, reassemble her scattered parts, and work in order
to live, without dreams or any plan for the days to
come. She cast her burden onto whatever might come;
whatever it was, she would not stand at its station,

waiting for the train that would take her away. She began each morning grateful to be alive, asking God for mercy upon those who had paid with their lives for a freedom they never tasted, and then she gave herself up to her work on the farm with Roujda, plowing, sowing, watering, and harvesting the crops. She and Roujda became like sisters, each supporting the other. No longer was Narjis the strange woman whose presence in the village gave rise to speculation and misgiving. People there came to know her as kin to Roujda, whom she accompanied on special occasions into the natural world that so abundantly provided for them—they would gather plants from which a profit could be made in the seasons when they flowered. She learned the names of plants previously unknown to her. Some were ingredients used in cooking; some were fruits offered to guests; some could be combined with flour and kneaded into bread dough; and others might be taken to market and sold—and in this, by degrees, she joined herself to the cooperation between Roujda and her son Shirwan.

Some days Dileir's wife Roseanne came. She was a lovely young woman, with the clear, rosy complexion of an angel. She didn't speak Arabic, so it was difficult for Narjis to interact with her. They would all head out together, early in the morning, in search of the plants that, during the harvest season, flourished in profusion on the mountain slopes and in the wide-open valleys. Some of these grew underground, and a type of trowel was required to uproot them;

the rest grew aboveground: edible thistles, nettles, mushrooms, rhubarb, rosehips, wild leeks, chanterelles, mallow, and wood sorrel. Each type of plant had a distinctive flavor, and there was a particular method for cooking each one or adding it to salads or preparing it as an appetizer; some, as well, had medicinal uses.

Thanks to Roujda, Narjis acquired a degree of expertise in plants and their uses. When she returned with Roujda and Shirwan from their expeditions, they would all set to cleaning the plants and packaging them. To this collection she would add whatever fruits and vegetables the farm had yielded, and then proceed to the market in the city with Shirwan and Dileir. She would get back around noon and wash and rub oil into her roughened hands, taking satisfaction in having become a worker, with friends who treated her as a member of the family. With them she partook of special occasions and times of celebration, when people put away their cares and opened the gates to the joys of the season.

You can't block the smile that finds its way out between sorrowing lips, any more than you can prevent the aroma of those seasons of joy as it rises into the air. By no means whatsoever could you slow the advent of those celebrations, no matter how high a wall of sorrows you tried to place in its way. To this people have been long accustomed. Thus they will wish you a happy holiday, even though they know happiness has passed by your door and will not visit you. They celebrate nature and its bounties, as if they may live forever, when it is this very place, this natural environment, that has stood witness to the deaths of those you love, upon its own soil.

Now it was *Nowruz*,[1] the Persian New Year, the first festival since Narjis was obliged to come to this place that she would go out into the florescence that adorned the slopes and valleys of the mountains of Kurdistan with every color of the rainbow. First, though, Roujda took her to Mawlawi Market in Sulaymaniyah, where they visited Azad, the most renowned tailor and designer in the city, who would fit her with a Kurdish costume suitable for this particular festival. In his workshop she saw numerous costumes resplendent with color, featuring embroidery of many hues and bespangled with beads, as well as ornaments of gold and silver. She chose a design that appealed also to Roujda, and to Azad himself.

The day she put on her new clothes to go out for the celebration, she tripped, nearly falling over the long hemline, which extended well past her feet. She only laughed, though, the smile finding its unimpeded way to her lips, and out she went to attend the festivities, where she was dazzled by what she saw. For as nature begins to renew its wardrobe, just so do people reinvigorate their own lives, putting on their fanciest clothing: embroidered, shimmering, in

---

1. Persian New Year is often celebrated in Iraqi Kurdish communities.

concert with nature in all its colors. They flock to the broad hillsides, the green mountains, the crystal-clear springs, where they dance the *dabke*, sing their songs, and eat of the bounty produced by their own hands. Afterward they go back home to await another day, on which they will resume the celebration: such is life in these mountain villages—although the loved ones lost to the bullet, to torture, to imprisonment, or to the ravages of chemical warfare are never forgotten; on the contrary, their imprint is indelible, they are stitched into the profoundest depths of the survivors, who memorialize them on occasions dedicated to mourning. At such times they go to the graves of their loved ones, or to the monuments they have erected in the memory of those they have never yet been able to trace. Narjis did likewise, placing at the foot of a holm oak a symbol to represent Yusef: a stone upon which his name was carved. She surrounded this with narcissus blossoms, which carried a double meaning. For this flower, her namesake, was of all flowers the one that had been chosen to represent the cities of the north, because of its effect upon the human spirit, its powerful fragrance, its abundant growth, and its many varieties appearing in the springtime. When she sat beside this memorial, she sensed Yusef's spirit hovering nearby. She spoke to him, whispering, "They cast you out of this life, but how could I cast you out of my heart? They made your body vanish, but I've made my heart a pillow for you. Our unfinished story will be filled out in the glow of my memory.

The soul they plucked from you hovers around me, looking after me. I will peel away the days until we meet again."

As Narjis rested in the shade of the holm oak after three hours of labor on the farm, leaning against its trunk, she contemplated her life: how it had been, and where she had ended up. She had come to this place looking for one thing and found something else— something that had sketched for her a way of living that had never occurred to her. Assailed by memories, she imagined Mukhlis Farouq in his bookshop, surprised by her arrival, taking a sharp breath and rising from behind his desk to greet her and ask her about her journey; she imagined telling him in detail about what had happened in her search for Yusef.

When Yusef himself appeared in the shadows of her memory, she stopped her mind from proceeding past the joys of love to what had become of their love, reaching far back into their childhood. She visualized the sandcastles on the banks of the river, how the water would rise and wash them away, how he and she would rebuild them . . . Her memories propelled her forward into thoughts of those passionate meetings, the recollection of that kiss that had not been repeated. The lines in her face relaxed, features opening like a flower, as she relived the tremors of love—albeit only as a reminiscence. Then, in spite of herself, she saw again that brute of a policeman, ready to place their love under arrest, there at Zawraa Park. Before he could thrust his finger into Yusef's face, however, Roujda's voice summoned her back to solid ground, with a stirring rendition of some lines from a song by Majid Al Mohandis,[2] a love song entreating the beloved for tenderness, offering a reminder that there has been no deceit: "The time apart is what betrays— wherever you are I'll come to you./ . . . If you could see me, my love, my sorrow would distress you."

Tears stood in Narjis's eyes, but Roujda turned the melancholy on its head, raising her voice in an Egyptian song that had been made famous in the eighties by a skilled singer known as Hanan: "Laugh, my friend, cheer up, and let us dream along with you . . . /Take safe-passage to joy, for what, in life, is more important?"

And with that Narjis's tears gave way to the smile that formed on her lips: there was yet relief in seeing other sides to life—in song and dance, in this green countryside upon which one lived, in those expeditions she now undertook fearlessly, with Roujda and her son Shirwan, to the open lands, the meadows so richly abundant.

Some meters off, the hens rested, sunning themselves after feeding, languid with no rooster in their midst—where had the rooster gone? Their eyes were fixed on the corner around which he had disappeared. When he peered out, with his red crest erect and his

2. Majid Al Mohandis (b. 1971): Iraqi-Saudi singer and composer.

showy feathers puffed up, they bestirred themselves and grew animated, dogging his steps wherever he went, clustering around him when he stopped. They watched and waited, but once again he would choose the white hen and have his way with her, eliciting from Narjis laughter so hearty it would reach Roujda's ears. Narjis would say to herself, "Either that rooster is a bigot, or at any rate he's in violation of the rights of his chosen mate's co-wives—they're all entitled to equal opportunity!"

Roujda hurried over carrying a yogurt-based dish of boiled edible thistle. She placed this before Narjis and asked her what it was that had made her laugh. Narjis told her the tale of the rooster and the hens, whereupon Roujda assured her that this rooster was more fair-minded than any other. What Narjis had observed, she said, was sheer coincidence, for the rooster mated with all the hens. At that very moment a cackling rose from the chickens, for the rooster, as if to prove the truth of Roujda's words, was mounting a brown hen. The women laughed.

When the rooster had finished his business, Roujda said cheerfully, "Roosters are more insatiable than men!"

This was something Narjis had not heard before, and she asked Roujda the basis for her assertion.

"I . . ." Roujda began confidently, then laughed when she spied a glimmer of doubt in Narjis's expression. "Stay as long as you can on the farm," she said, "and take note of how often the rooster pairs off with his hens. You'll find that a man can't attend to his women so often as a rooster can!"

Narjis laughed out loud, and Roujda said, "That's it! Cheer up, laugh—in laughter there is life, whereas tears are the end of life's race. The past is over and done with, while the future can't be known—all we have is the moment we're in."

Narjis realized that Roujda never talked about her own past, nor did she dwell on what the future might hold. She confided no secrets other than those that came out by chance. She was a woman living in the present, in word and in deed. She arranged her life as ongoing labor, punctuated by laughter and her pleasure in knickknacks.

"See here, Narjis," she said. "What do you say I get another rooster, so we can see what our buddy here does?"

The following day, she came home from the market with a new rooster. Narjis was still out working on the farm, so Roujda called her, and they stood in front of the chicken coop. She scattered chickenfeed and set the rooster down so that he could share the feast. The original rooster stopped eating and stared at the new one, who was applying himself to his own food as if he hadn't eaten in several days. Each time the distance between them began to close, the first rooster lengthened it again with a shriek. After eating and drinking, the second rooster approached one of the hens, but before he could make a move on her the first rooster advanced on him. Puffing up his neck feathers and spreading his wings, he engaged his rival in a fierce battle, trying to get at his eyes and gouge them out. He pecked relentlessly at the other rooster, aiming for everything in sight, or leaping onto the other bird's back and thrusting his sharp beak into its neck, until he had bloodied the creature. The new rooster fell to the ground under this assault, covered in his own blood.

Roujda seemed happy with this battle, unlike her hens. The hens were distressed by the defeat of a new rooster whose arrival had pleased them at first, for perhaps their conjugal rights would have been better fulfilled than they were under the reign of their proud master, with his puffed-up feathers and his arrogant stare.

Roujda picked up the vanquished rooster and went to tend to his wounds. She decided that she would build a second coop at the far end of the farm, and bring him a number of hens. "You see, Narjis," she said, "how the rooster defends his 'honor,' while there are men who drive their women to dishonor."

16

Like a wild stallion, unstoppable, the days ran on, bearing all creation forward on time's serrated edge; days became months, from which the dry and barren years take shape. Stories proliferate, becoming beloved faces, from that part of the memory which settles in the heart before the mind.

News of the nation was for the most part not encouraging, as if time were proceeding in a direction opposite to the progress of life. As if the helmets upon men's heads were an impalpable symbol, something that must adhere to the skull; as if olive drab were all the rage—a mark of distinction. Dreams, meanwhile, were nothing but a muddle—why have dreams? Others will dream dreams for you and bring you a tomorrow consisting of what someone else has seen fit to arrange for you. You are helpless to dream: It is they who dream upon feather pillows, while you can only put on your helmet, with all its infinitely varied nightmarish decorations. Of whom then would you dream, and why? Dreams are a luxury you can't afford. You want an interval of peace and safety in your life?

Whoever told you your life belonged to you? No, it belongs to the sovereign—he alone decides when you may breathe to keep on living, and when your breath will cease. It is you who must die, while it is his right to live longer than the Seven Sleepers, who slept for three hundred years. But on every life, however long, a term is set—even if the end does not come for ages. Better this than that it should last forever.

And so it seemed strange that the world should be convulsed: Had the bull shifted its horns and dropped its burden on the earth? Had the earth been split by a terrible earthquake? Or was Judgment Day, of which we had heard but in whose coming we had not believed, now upon us? Oh, mythical bull, why did your horns not move before now? Before bodies were shattered and burned by all the years of warfare that have gone before? Before the vanishing of those who vanished? Before youths' and infants' arms and legs were mutilated, leaving them to live as amputees, permanently traumatized?

But the thing happened, and its occurrence was at last announced. It was like when something falls that, all your life, you believed was fixed in the ground, immovable, proof against uprooting by violent storms, fixed in and upon you, around, above, and beneath you: a person who could terrorize you with his eyes; whose henchmen patrolling the streets were ghouls who found their way under your skin until you scarcely recognized it, while you lived in a state of anxiety in your own house, as well as on the streets you walked; who caught up with you in your bed, your sleep, your dreams; who would tax you for breathing the same air he breathed; who sowed fear in you and stripped you of your soul until you turned against your own homeland and sought out any means by which you might escape to some other country—you could do without your country's hawthorn and its figs, for all you wanted was to live in peace before the sharks devoured you . . . but the sharks were brought down at last.

At last the earthquake struck, struck with a resounding crash. The sultan's throne collapsed, toppled by the first blow of the hammer. The earth was ablaze with gunfire and missile strikes, and the leader disappeared—he whose lips had never ceased those declarations of bravado and heroism they spouted day and night, by which so many unfortunate soldiers had fallen along the highway and byways of death, melting like ore, and vanishing in the blink of an eye, as if their mothers had never borne them.

Everything went to pieces in short order; there was no country left: the president had disappeared, the army gone up in smoke; the ramparts of terror had crumbled. Terrifying records that documented the crimes committed over the years emerged.

In other developments, the proliferation of satellite dishes occurred with amazing rapidity. Roujda, roused by the shocking events depicted on her neighbors' television screens, bought a dish, which Dileir installed for her. Secrets were secret no longer—all that had once been concealed was dug up and exposed. There were tons of documents that had been burned by the authorities before they fled, and tons that had come into the possession of the American occupiers. Still others were in the hands of professional thieves, and, likewise, thousands of documents were offered up, by the roadsides, for sale at any price.

At the outset, those in power, secure in the certainty of their own immortality, had recorded and photographed their crimes so as to enjoy their victims' torment. They documented everything: executions, disappearances, methods of killing and of savage torture, as well as displacement of civilians and the demolition of their homes. By way of these documents many mass graves also came to light. People rushed to get to the security headquarters, the prisons, the detention centers, the intelligence offices, and the party outposts, where they ferreted out secret files and extracted the dismal facts, so that they would not perish. There were those who saw a son or brother or father drawing his last breaths; or being blown up by means of dynamite placed on his chest; or thrown to vicious dogs that had been starved for several days; or laid out, blindfolded and bound hand and foot, to have his tongue cut out, followed by his head, which would then be snatched up, held on high, and dangled before his assembled kinfolk so as to be a lesson to them; or he might be placed, still alive, on a slab, to have cement poured on him—his eyes still in place, so that he might be witness, until his last moment, his last breath, of his own fate: to be buried alive in cement. Crimes inconceivable to human minds: all of this appeared on videodisks, some of which were shown, via satellite, on people's screens.

Narjis planted herself in front of the television to follow the news. Planes filled the skies, while gunfire both celebratory and lethal poured out relentlessly; explosions and corpses were all over the place—government agencies, military barracks, safe-houses, hospitals, poultry farms, marketplaces, mosques, and schools. Above all there was confusion, but when all was said and done she understood that the wheels of time would not restore the regime as it had been before, and that a new era was center stage now, although it was still in its infancy, the shape it would assume as yet unknown. A sign of the general trajectory of things was offered on the day that American tanks reached Baghdad, and a soldier climbed on top of one of them to drape an American flag around the neck of the president's statue in Paradise Square; when the masses objected, he replaced it with an Iraqi flag. Then he wrapped an iron chain around the statue's neck, so that a tank on the opposite side could pull it. The president's monument resisted as long as possible, before crashing down from its paradise, leaving behind on the pedestal a pair of hollow feet.

The president vanished, and afterwards so did his billboards, becoming heaps of rubbish in the blink of an eye; all means possible were used toward their removal from every city in Iraq: hatchets, axes, bulldozers, and tanks, as if the people were exacting their revenge against the prohibitions that had stolen time from them and robbed them of their lives.

Then came the looting and pillaging, everywhere from the palaces of the deposed authorities to the government agencies, whether civil or military. They carried off everything that could be carried off: furniture, appliances, personal effects, paintings, items of decor, money, and documents. But what caused real distress was that the National Museum was plundered of all its treasures and major acquisitions.

Narjis and Roujda followed this terrible report, as the glassed-in display cases were shattered, and the thieves' deft hands reached in to seize whatever was of the greatest value: thousands of antiquities, including cylinder seals, coins, and gold jewelry dating from the Sumerian, Babylonian, and Assyrian eras. The history of a country, a civilization, dating back to the furthest reaches of time was ruthlessly plundered. These were thefts that could only have been carried out by skilled and organized thieves who had been waiting for the green light. They got it, and they committed their crime before the eyes of the American soldiers.

Roujda could do nothing to stem the flow of Narjis's tears—they fell from her eyes and from her heart—for Roujda wept as well. Then she tried to console Narjis. "What are relics and antiquities," she said, "compared to what happens to human beings? You see the bodies, displayed by satellite without regard for whose they were, without any accounting for people's feelings—didn't you see the mass graves that have begun to turn up?"

Dear God, the staggering number of mortal remains! How could it be that in one grave there were more than fifteen bodies? The first grave was discovered in al-Mahawil: children, women, men old and young. Knowing nothing, families of victims scrambled to dig, exhuming bones in search of personal belongings that they might recognize. In this way, evidence pointing to the perpetrators of such butchery was lost. Then other graves began to appear all over the country: north, south, east, and west. And after this, Narjis, you weep over stones?

The borders had opened, for the guards, fleeing, had left them, letting in hordes from all over who came to sow terror in the minds of the people and spread massacre and mayhem: belts packed with explosives or cars rigged to blow up, detonating streets and marketplaces, buildings such as restaurants and mosques, as well as wedding and funeral pavilions.

A few days later, as Narjis watched, her blood ran cold. She stared hard at the picture shown on the television screen, listening to the report being delivered by a broadcaster on one of the Arabic channels concerning the perpetrator of the dreadful explosion that had occurred in Baghdad's al-Tayaran Square. The terrorist, driving a pickup truck, had approached a group of unfortunate day-laborers and signaled to them, so that they hurried over, jostling one another as they came, for each one hoped for a chance at a job that might ensure that his family would eat that day. It was normal for men to come in their vehicles and take three or four workers, but the driver of the pickup shouted at the top of his voice, "Don't shove! Climb onto the truck, all of you—we have a big project." What sort of "big project" could this be? Not one of them asked any such question, for hunger is a beast. They picked up their tools and settled in the bed of the pickup. But before the truck could proceed any farther, the terrorist blew himself up, and body parts flew everywhere. It was a ghastly explosion, whose toll included dozens of construction workers and passersby.

Narjis was thunderstruck, not only by the enormity of the death toll and the bodies strewn everywhere, but by the image of the terrorist that filled the screen, and whose name was now widely known. She covered her mouth with her hand so as not to cry out, for the man was her uncle, her mother's brother Bandar, who had come back from America to seek his paradise in the bodies of poor and the innocent. Narjis stopped her voice, so her cry would not be heard by Roujda, who at that moment was preparing lunch, but she took not one bite of food when it was served. She was weeping inconsolably, and with each of Roujda's attempts to soothe her she cried the more. Roujda threatened to disconnect the satellite for a respite from these calamities. She turned off the television and urged Narjis to go out with her into the countryside and gather wild plants, but Narjis declined. In the state she was in, nature held no colors for her anymore.

At first, Narjis turned the thing over in her own mind. Then she discussed it with Roujda, Dileir, and Keke Tariq. She was torn between a desire to return to Baghdad—now that what had held her back was no longer a factor—and the possibility of staying in Sulaymaniyah with her "family," who sheltered her, and in whose midst she had found affection and compassion. Keke Tariq and Dileir were opposed to a decision to go back, while Roujda took a position in the middle, suggesting that Narjis go back for a visit, then return to Sulaymaniyah. In the end, everyone agreed as to a visit, but Keke Tariq objected to the timing. Baghdad, he said, was unsafe at the moment, and not a day passed without explosions and kidnappings and armed robberies. Gangs roamed and pounced, unchecked. She must, therefore, postpone the visit until things calmed down. He promised that, at the right time, he would help her make the journey.

So she held off. But the protracted wait exceeded her patience, for things did not calm down. The Americans had deposed one individual, and toppled a nation, with no thought for what would replace it. Perhaps the replacement was this bedlam they referred to as "creative chaos," and when that came to an end, at some distant point in time, they would assemble a sort of system that would serve their own interests?

As day followed day, Narjis began to revisit her calculations, perhaps to persuade herself to follow Keke Tariq's advice. To whom, she asked herself, and to what losses would she be returning? The answer seemed perverse to her—or maybe she didn't want to acknowledge it even to herself. Something of her old determination held fast, but it broke down when she connected with the deepest parts of herself. At last she admitted it: that it was simply the places she held in memory that she wanted to revisit. For they were her treasury, fresh sustenance in days of want. Her desire—though it might seem like a whim—was to tread once more that ground, those paths; to sit in the shade of the tree in Zawraa Park; to knock on the door belonging to the present owners of what was once her mother's house and ask permission to go up to the roof, on the pretext that she had left something there; to proceed from there to Mutanabbi Street and go to Mukhlis Farouq's bookstore, to ask him whether he'd found Yusef's family and given them the document recording his execution.

But time was not on the side of gratified wishes, she had to face it. Be guided by reason, woman, not by your feelings, and if you have something in hand now, don't waste it.

Her desire stayed hidden, for the dark tunnel was longer than she had thought, in Baghdad's night.

17

Narjis developed the habit of distracting herself with work, for relief from the oppressiveness of sad memories, and the images that assailed her when she was at rest. No share of her memories belonged to Mu'nis al-Shaa'ir; even had she lived her life a thousand times over she would have dismissed him without a second thought. She exhausted her body so that it might rest during the nighttime hours, but then the night would cast her back into her memories once more, presenting her with a number of questions that kept her awake: What are you doing here, Narjis? In this place you are soulless—will you wait for old age, so far from the places in which your soul resides? Here you are, leaving the years behind you, with no dreams, no prospects, no provisions to take with you on your life's final journey. You didn't think, at the outset, of what would happen when your fingers betrayed you, and thus you've got nothing left to hold onto. You have one hope now, just one, that's igniting your desire to go back. You try to extinguish it, but it won't be put out. So what to do but carry it through? Why are you deluding yourself, when most of what matters to you is there—the places, the memories, some kind of work having to do with restoring people's rights? And if, once there, you don't find your soul, you can come back and seek it here.

She held at bay the desire that engulfed her, to keep it from digging in deeper, looming larger in her mind. She managed it for a while but the longing to return to Baghdad pressed itself upon her. She could not go on anymore, persuading herself to postpone it and postpone it again, waiting for some faint sign of a calm that never came. Day after day, month after month, her longing grew like a seed struggling to find itself an opening that will let it out into the sunshine. Then it began to weigh upon her like a boulder she was trying to push back into its original place. Thus her desire was transformed into a determination she could not expel from her mind, no matter the warnings with which Roujda, Dileir, and Keke Tariq confronted her.

Again they ran through the risks with her: Chaos stalked the land; the Americans were occupying the country; murderous gangs filled the streets; new and bizarre political parties had sprung up and were fighting one another over who should take the stage; militias, in the absence of an organized state, were unfettered. "This is not what we struggled for, not what we were hoping—we've lost our compass and sunk the ship. We don't know what will happen tomorrow or after that."

But she faced them down with her own resolve. "I'm determined to go to Baghdad," she said. "If no one assists me, I'll chance it on my own, just as I did the first time."

This time Narjis would not be looking for keys to open the gates, for the gates were ajar throughout the furthest reaches of the north and south, and thieves roamed freely, exultant, as well as dealers in death. "Who made you Pharaoh?" they said. "There was no one to stop me," Pharaoh replied.

Narjis put on thick clothing, with a woolen shawl over her shoulders, as she began her journey of return on a cold morning, heavily overcast. She knew she was proceeding with no surety. She left the villages, forests, farms and fields, mountains and waterfalls, sensing that she would not see these places again.

Keke Tariq accompanied her far enough to leave her at a garage where three taxis were waiting. None of her fellow travelers were venturing to Baghdad or any other city in the central or southern part of the country, but Keke Tariq had made an agreement with another driver whom he knew and trusted. He was standing at the back of the garage, waiting for Keke Tariq, who pressed him to look after Narjis, to take her where she wanted to go, and to help her if she decided to come back. "Go in safety," he said to her, and with that the car set off.

It was as if the land was not itself: bomb craters, husks of vehicles, and cars reduced to cinders all along the road, as well as burned trees, decapitated palms, demolished buildings, abandoned houses, banners for political parties no one had heard of, posters and billboards featuring men of every sort, every description: wearing turbans or Iraqi side-caps or kaffiyehs, or else bareheaded—their eyes followed Narjis the whole way. The air was suffused with the odor of gunpowder, and of coagulated blood.

Dread lurked everywhere, inarticulate, as if fear itself feared what the coming days would bring. American tanks, both instilling and evincing a sense of alarm, proceeded rapidly, or else cruised the streets, their muzzles, those hateful weapons, trained on the citizens.

An odd thing—she read a line of verse by the poet al-Ma'arri[1] written in colored paint on the wall of a ruined house, like an ominous message directed at her: "Be not misled—this is an aimless journey / Robbing the soul of sweet slumber."

Checkpoints where roads divided were manned by soldiers not wearing khaki, who stopped cars and scrutinized papers before allowing them to pass.

Incredulous, Narjis stared: an American soldier, his weapon drawn, standing beside his tank, which was surmounted by other American soldiers. He signaled the car to stop. Beside him was an Iraqi youth, who served as his translator. The driver presented his

1. Abu al-'Alaa al-Ma'arri (973–1057): Syrian poet and philosopher.

papers, and a few minutes later the soldier gestured to let him proceed, saying in English, "Welcome."

He was the one to bid "welcome" to the country's own citizens, as if he'd been born of this clay and they were the visitors whose business was suspect? The car passed more checkpoints and more burned-out buildings. The already-numerous ruts and pot-holes proliferated, and the driver was forced to find a way around several tall cement barriers in order to achieve, at last, the gateway to Baghdad. The driver conducted his vehicle along routes variously tortu-ous or broken, sometimes coming to roads that were blocked altogether, so that he had to turn around. Looming above all this destruction were signs and pictures and billboards of the new leaders, shown larger than life. These dominated the government es-tablishments, the institutions, the streets, the plazas, even the checkpoints. The sky over Baghdad was still gloomy, the faces of its inhabitants grim, despairing, full of confusion. Much had changed for the worse, to the point where it seemed as though life lay in the palm of a monster more lunatic than its predecessor.

"Please," said Narjis, "I'd like to go first to Mu-tanabbi Street."

"We'll cross the Moatham Gate Bridge shortly," said the driver, "and go from there to Rashid Street— that's if they'll let us through."

"And if they don't?"

"We'll look for another route."

The sky was an accumulation of clouds and smoke, the atmosphere uneasy. The crowd in the city was dense, and security barricades were many—innumerable, the streets cut off like severed limbs. The checkpoints chopped them up to effect a single passageway, which would be simpler to control. Many roads were closed off entirely, blocked by piles of concrete, so that drivers were forced into branching streets to reach their destinations. Neighborhoods were isolated from one another by walls separating them. There was smoke rising from a building on the other side of the Tigris River, near Medical City, while American soldiers stood ready at the checkpoint that had been set up on the western end of the bridge. Everyone was subject to search and inspection, to doubt and suspicion over belief and trust. After a good deal of inconvenience, the car crossed the Moatham Gate Bridge, but was then unable to turn right, toward where the old Ministry of Defense building stood, on the road that led to the entrance to Rashid Street, for heaps of concrete and barbed wire had been placed there before the checkpoint. Voices issued warnings—directives to turn around; machine guns were ready to deal with anyone who disobeyed orders. There was nothing the driver could do but set a course for the entrance to Republic Street, to wind his way toward al-Maedan Square, and from there to Rashid Street. But another checkpoint brought him to a halt at the entrance to al-Maedan Square, and this time he wasn't allowed to pass.

"How can we get to Mutanabbi Street, then?" the driver asked the guard at the checkpoint, whose face was masked.

"Is there anyone who still buys books these days?" he replied, with evident sarcasm.

"I'm trying to get to my brother," said Narjis. "He works there."

"Cars are forbidden to go through," the officer said, his tone peremptory. "You can't park anywhere in this area, either," he added.

The prohibitions mounting, Narjis summoned her courage and told the driver, "Brother, you've done your job. Don't worry about me—I'll get there on foot."

He proposed taking her to some family members of his in al-Za'franiya, where she might rest after the fatigue of the journey, and come another day to Mutanabbi Street. But she was full of a strange resolve, and declined, asking only for his telephone number, as she might need it some other time. And with that they parted ways.

She walked over rutted ground, anxiously, at an urgent pace, as if in flight from some obscure pursuer, stepping over puddles left by the rain. She still remembered everything, and as she walked on toward Mutanabbi Street she was accompanied by the voice of Umm Kulthoum that had once issued from the coffeehouse bearing her name. Everything seemed alien now, even the faces of the passersby. Narjis smelled the odor of death, and sensed spirits hovering mournfully; she heard the noise of explosions that had not yet been set off; murderers seemed to beckon to her, hidden in corners where they lay in ambush, with their meat-cleavers and concealed pistols and belts packed with explosives.

Wooden carts, once seemingly extinct in city streets, emerged from oblivion to announce their presence, coming and going at will. She was startled by a man pulling his donkey by a rope, the beast laden with odds and ends, and by the vendors' stalls whose owners occupied the broken sidewalks. Many shops and restaurants were closed, and there were piles of garbage, so the whole area stank with decay. There were ruined walls, with pieces of cement and brick-work lying about—doubtless these were the walls of ancient buildings that had collapsed on account of the frequent explosions.

Before proceeding by way of Rashid Street to Mukhlis Farouq's bookshop, she drew back as if she had forgotten something. She stood still, listening. Where was that voice, the one that could be heard at all hours, even in the middle of the night, coming from Umm Kulthoum Café? Why had the Lady[2] abandoned the café? A memory came back to Narjis,

2. The Lady: the renowned and much-revered Egyptian singer Umm Kulthoum (d. 1975), here referred to by a word that, while it can mean "lady," also connotes mastery, for she was and is regarded as an unparalleled vocal artist.

of that day when she had entered the café with Yusef. It was a challenge they had undertaken, when they decided to flout the rule according to which the only Umm Kulthoum fans who frequented the place were men. Suddenly all eyes were upon them. The gurgle of the narghiles stopped, likewise the clatter of dominoes, but the voice of the Lady, singing, "I can't forget you," did not stop. Narjis and Yusef sat in a corner, replete with delight, the object of the astonished gazes that remained fastened upon them. It might be that one of the other patrons took their bizarre arrival as a piece of effrontery, or someone else was about to protest, and someone demanded that either the owner of the café should eject them or he'd take it on himself to do so. For how could a woman invade a world belonging to men, how could she, accompanied by her lover, challenge the tradition that prevailed? But no one openly raised any objection. Little by little, the rattle of dominoes started up again and the narghiles resumed their gurgling. With the lyrics of the song in the background, the two of them drank their tea, and then left, feeling triumphant.

Where had the Lady's voice gone? Who, after all these years, had caused it to vanish? And why were the eyes of the men in the street fixed on her as if they beheld a woman who had descended from some other planet?

She edged along the sidewalk, spurred on by the hope of reaching Mukhlis Farouq's bookstore and seeing him, of picking up once more the rhythm of their shared memories. She would occupy the chair, the one that, out of four altogether, Yusef had preferred to sit on. The other three, all brown, had resembled one another, while the fourth featured upholstery striped in white, black, and red. The sidewalk was taken up with the piles of goods laid out upon it, including packages of fruits and vegetables, plastic shoes, and used clothing. The cries of the vendors and the general din filled her ears. Porters and children begging—the orphans of terrorism, no doubt—importuned passersby, while amputees made their way by means of wheeled devices or prosthetic limbs, faces anxious, eyes lusterless. All this chaos in the street that seemed as though it had been dealt a pitiless wound, stabbed to its heart.

She passed under the old portico—it was noontime. She breathed the smoke, glancing now and then at the ancient buildings, featuring the traditional oriel window known as *shansula*. They had aged more than they should have, their vividness dimmed, tainting the memory of them. She almost doubted that she was actually on Rashid Street, the jewel of Baghdad, so much did it resemble to her an old man exhausted from a long journey, overcome with illness, with nothing before him but to await the moment of his death, grieving that there was no one to escort him to his final resting place, as would befit his splendid, his venerable past.

She wondered where the aroma of Al-Sayyid's Cake Shop[3] had gone. And where were the shops selling silver crafts? And did people still quench their thirst with a fruit drink from Hajj Zabala's establishment?[4] Did the movie theaters still have patrons? And were there any unveiled women . . . where were the unveiled women? The only women she saw were wrapped in black abayas or jubbahs, and their heads were covered. Were the bookstores and stalls and sidewalk displays of Mutanabbi Street still crowded with books and customers? Was the voice of Naim al-Shatari still to be heard, calling out to announce first editions? Or was a book no longer the ideal companion? She could almost, imagining days gone by, detect from afar the aroma of paper, as she proceeded toward her goal, invoking Yusef's face—Yusef, a nearly palpable presence; she could almost hear the voice of Umm Kulthoum, which rose up from deep within her, despite all she saw before her: "Years passed like seconds in the embrace of your love / And if I were able to love again, I would love you."

But then a man shouted at her. Umm Kulthoum's voice shivered and vanished. "Cover your head, woman!" yelled the man.

3. Al-Sayyid's Cake Shop: famous bakery established in 1937 by al-Sayyid Hussein Ali al-Darraji al-Samira'i.
4. Hajj Zabala's Refreshments: popular establishment on Rashid Street, still in existence.

She turned in his direction, and wrapped her shawl around her head, without even considering what she might say to him in reply. The fear in her bowels that she had believed gone, once the regime fell, began to creep back in a different form, emanating from that man, with his beard, who still held her in the glare of his disapproval, making sure she wouldn't bare her head once more. To escape his glowering visage, she had to stop in front of a cart offering used clothing for sale, on the pretext of intending to buy something.

All at once a hue and cry went up, people running in all directions, among them a man pursued by policemen who were trying to lay hold of him. Shots rang out, there was a lot of shouting, and miscellaneous objects were flung about as people pushed and shoved one another in the confusion. Everyone sought a safe corner or tried to slip into one of the alleyways branching off the main street before death could waylay them. A young man with an artificial leg who was trying to get to safety fell down; another helped him up, and they hurried off.

Narjis, conscious of danger, was at a loss. She found herself stuck where she was, hemmed in against the wall of a small shop, along with a group of other bewildered people to whom the general alarm had given no opportunity of taking to their heels. The man who was fleeing the police raced toward them. A child extricated himself from the throng and ran, disappearing swiftly into a nearby alley. His mother screamed and rushed after him; she had covered half the distance when the man on the run shouted at the top of his lungs, "God is great!" and detonated his explosive belt. Human bodies, as well as fragments of human and metal and stone were flung higher than the roofs and balconies of the nearby buildings, and into the street. Glass storefronts shattered. Heads rolled, amid disembodied fingers and feet, while flesh adhered to the walls and the asphalt. Dreams went up in smoke; departing spirits drifted uncertainly, not knowing why they had left their bodies. Fires broke out; the façades of some of the old buildings crumbled and collapsed. An artificial leg dangled from the iron rail of a balcony, half of which had fallen to the ground. Before the clouds of smoke could clear or the death-fires be extinguished, so that the gathering-up of fragments could begin, a man's voice burst out in terror, like something erupting from a giant's throat, "Everyone, run for your lives! There's going to be another explosion! Run! Run! Run! R—"

Glossary

abaya. A cloak-like wrap; frequently of wool but may be composed of other fabric.

araq. A strong alcoholic drink, distilled from dates or from anise.

dabke. A traditional line-dance popular in much of the Levant.

dishdasha. An ankle-length, long-sleeved garment worn by men, particularly in the Arabian Gulf countries.

doina. A Kurdish fried dish consisting of yogurt, wheat, and various flavorings.

gaiwa. A type of traditional hand-crafted Kurdish shoe.

jubbah. A cloak, or long outer garment, open in front, with wide sleeves.

khamsin. A sandstorm.

kaffiyeh. A square scarf, usually cotton, sometimes featuring a pattern indicating tribal or nationalist affiliation, and frequently held in place on the head by a type of cord known as an *agal* that is made from camel- or goat-hair.

masto. A simple, yogurt-based dish found in Kurdistan and Iran.

narghile. A device for smoking tobacco (or sometimes hashish) consisting of a flexible or bamboo pipe attached to a bottle-like receptacle filled with water, through which smoke is drawn to filter and cool it; also variously known as hubbly-bubbly, *hookah*, *gouza*, or *shisha*.

shansula. A type of traditional, oriel-style window.

tarhkhina. A traditional Kurdish wheat-based dish cooked with vegetables and spices.

Originally from Baghdad, Hadiya Hussein began publishing fiction in 1993. She is the author of more than a dozen novels and short-story collections. Her first novel to appear in English was *Beyond Love*, published in Arabic in 2004; the English translation was brought out by Syracuse University Press in 2012. *Waiting for the Past* was first published in Arabic under the title *What Will Come*, in 2017.

Barbara Romaine began teaching and translating Arabic in the early 1990s. She has previously published translations of five novels, as well as numerous shorter works (poetry, short stories, and essays), which have appeared in various literary journals. In 2011 she placed second for the Saif Ghobash Banipal Prize for Arabic Literary Translation. In 2007 and 2015 her work was supported by fellowships in translation from the National Endowment for the Arts.

Born in the United States, Iraqi artist Maysaloun Faraj (cover illustration) received a BSc in architecture from Baghdad University in 1978, and later went on to pursue her artistic aspirations in London and Paris. Committed to raising the profile of Iraqi artists—through her publications, for example, as well as the establishment of Aya Gallery in London—she is also a distinguished artist in her own right. Her work is vividly expressive of a broad range of human experience, from the effects of war on the people of Iraq to global responses to the COVID-19 pandemic.